Dark

DEATH DAY

by

ANTHONY MASTERS

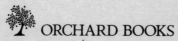 ORCHARD BOOKS

To Mary Hamley
who shared the vision

ORCHARD BOOKS
96 Leonard Street, London EC2A 4XD
Orchard Books Australia
14 Mars Road, Lane Cove, NSW 2066
First published in Great Britain in 2000
Paperback original
Text © Anthony Masters, 2000
The right of Anthony Masters to be identified as the
author of this work has been asserted by him
in accordance with the Copyright,
Designs and Patents Act, 1988.
A CIP catalogue record for this book is
available from the British Library.
ISBN 1 86039 945 2
1 3 5 7 9 10 8 6 4 2
Printed in Great Britain

1

Sunday, 6th

It's my birthday on Friday — I'm going to be 13
at last, a teenager! I'm not having a party or
anything, but I am going on a theatre trip with
the English department which I've been looking
forward to for ages. I just wish I had a friend
to share it with. If only Jane was still my
friend. I hate seeing her with Dawn and Sue —
I can't help feeling jealous and angry. They've
really turned her against me, and now she just
makes fun of me, calling me fat and stupid. I
wish we could have stayed at our old school —
then none of this would have happened and I'd
still have Jane.

Lucy saw Jane in the girls' toilets. She was facing
away from her, standing by the wash basins but not
looking up into the mirrors. They were so cracked
and dirty she probably wouldn't have seen Lucy
anyway.

Jane had one sleeve of her thick school sweater

3

rolled up. She was shivering slightly.

Lucy could see that her arm was covered in biro squiggles, and at first she couldn't work out what they were. But suddenly she realised the squiggles were answers to the history exam. Jane was going to cheat. She had been away ill for a couple of weeks and although she'd been sent work home, she obviously hadn't caught up.

As Lucy walked across to the basins, Jane hurriedly pulled her jersey down without a word. She hardly ever spoke to Lucy anyway, so that wasn't much of a surprise.

They couldn't have been more different. Jane was popular, as good at lessons as she was at games. Lucy was shy, didn't have many friends and was bad at games. Jane was tall and slim, with lovely long straight blonde hair and a flawless complexion. Lucy was short, with dull mousy hair, and considering herself plain and uninteresting, she never even tried to look good. But she just lacked confidence, always seeing herself in the worst possible light. She was actually very warm-hearted, with a lively sense of humour, but no one ever really saw it.

The day of the exam was cold and the hall was freezing. The students were wearing as many heavy sweaters as they could and the Head had turned a blind eye to uniform. Of course, thought Lucy, Jane's rollneck sweater with its baggy sleeves was absolutely ideal for covering up her arm. Her cheating arm.

Lucy watched as Jane casually flicked up her sleeve, yawning slightly and stretching, taking in the answers at a flash. As far as Lucy was concerned, Jane had always seemed honest and straightforward. Now she was cheating and Lucy could hardly believe the evidence of her own eyes. It was so unfair. Why should Jane get away with it? Suppose she got better marks than anyone else? Lucy felt a surge of resentment against her old best friend who had so cruelly turned against her, and for an instant she wanted to punish her. Before she knew it, she'd made up her mind to tell someone, although if she'd thought longer she wouldn't have done anything of the kind. It wasn't in her nature. Telling on Jane was a gut reaction, an impulse she couldn't stop.

Lucy hung back as the students filed out of the draughty hall, heading for the warm and stuffy canteen. Slowly she approached the desk where

Mrs Greenway was counting the papers.

'Miss.'

'Yes, Lucy?'

'Could I have a word?'

'Can it wait?'

'Not really.'

'Very well. Come to the office then.'

Mrs Greenway had been the invigilator for the exam and she was also a deputy head. She seemed just the right person for Lucy to approach. She slammed the door of her cluttered office, looking impatient. 'What is it?'

Lucy suddenly wanted to stop herself blurting it all out but somehow she couldn't. 'Someone was cheating.'

'*What?*' Mrs Greenway looked horrified.

'Cheating in the exam.'

'Who?'

Lucy paused, knowing that she might regret what she was going to say for a very long time. Then it came tumbling out.

'Jane Crow.'

The instant she said it Lucy was horrified. She'd dropped Jane right in it and there was no way she could take it back. Desperately she searched for something to say. Could she pretend it was a joke? That it was someone else – not

Jane? But it was already too late.

'Rubbish. Jane wouldn't do a thing like that. She's a really decent girl –' Mrs Greenway, tall and hawk-like, looked at Lucy as if she wasn't decent at all. 'Now, why are you making trouble like this?'

'I'm not, Miss,' said Lucy. Mrs Greenway wasn't being fair. Neither was Jane. Why didn't anyone ever take her seriously? Sudden indignation overtook her. 'She had the answers written on her arm.'

'Don't talk nonsense.'

'Why don't you go and see before she washes them off?' demanded Lucy. 'It's not fair on the rest of us.'

Mrs Greenway gazed at Lucy with gathering contempt. Then she sighed and said, 'All right, I'll look into it. I'll page her on the tannoy.'

'Don't raise her suspicions,' Lucy advised her, more confident now. 'Say you've got some lost property of hers. If you don't –'

'I don't need you to tell me what to do,' said Mrs Greenway, annoyed. 'Have you told anyone else?'

'Not yet.'

'Well, don't.'

'Are you going to say I told on her?' asked Lucy fearfully.

'No. Now let me investigate.'

Lucy hurried out of Mrs Greenway's office, shivering in the cold air of the corridor. What *had* she done? But she knew what she'd done. She'd done something terrible.

Lucy went into her next lesson and sat tensely, trying to make sense of her actions. What was going to happen to Jane? Had she managed to get the biro off her arm? Whatever the outcome, her betrayal was a dreadful thing and she wished she had never gone to Mrs Greenway in the first place. She knew she'd now set a course of action in motion that she couldn't control. How could she have told on Jane?

At break, she walked uneasily into the playground, only to see Mrs Greenway beckoning to her.

'Give me a second, Lucy. I don't think you handed in your homework, did you?'

Lucy was about to say that she most definitely had, when she saw the look in Mrs Greenway's eyes and quickly bit back her words. Obviously, the homework accusation was only a pretence, a means of attracting her attention without arousing suspicion.

She approached Mrs Greenway uneasily, as if

they were both acting in a play and she couldn't remember all her lines.

'I want a word with you,' Mrs Greenway said. 'You'd better come to my office.'

Once inside, Mrs Greenway closed the door but didn't ask Lucy to sit down. She came straight to the point. 'I'm sorry to say you were right.'

'You mean –'

'Jane had some of the answers to the exam written on her arm.'

'She owned up?' asked Lucy stupidly.

'She didn't have much choice, did she?' Mrs Greenway gave her an impatient glance.

'Did I do wrong?' asked Lucy.

'No.'

Should I have kept quiet?'

'Of course not. It wouldn't be fair on the others, would it? But I do suggest you're very discreet now. Jane's a popular girl.'

Lucy nodded, relieved that Mrs Greenway had given her a certain justification for what she had done. It wasn't fair. It wasn't fair on anyone. But inside she felt terrified. 'What's going to happen to her?'

Mrs Greenway frowned. 'Jane has her own

punishment. Her exam paper has been automatically disqualified and soon everyone will find out and she'll be disgraced. I'm going to suspend her for a day so that she can get her thoughts in order.'

'Will you – will you tell Jane who gave her away?'

'Of course not. But if I were you, I'd keep a low profile. That'll be all,' said Mrs Greenway dismissively.

2

Tuesday, 8th

It's 4.00am in the morning and I can't sleep.
I just keep tossing and turning and worrying –
I can't believe I did it...I grassed on Jane.
I wanted to be Jane's friend again. Not her
enemy. Now she'll hate me for ever. If only
I could have yesterday all over again...I just
acted on the spur of the moment. But there's
no going back now. I can't bear the thought of
school in the morning – it's going to be awful.

There was no public announcement, but the news
filtered through. The first Lucy heard of Jane's
disgrace was the following day when she came out
of the cloakroom and overheard a group of
students in her year discussing the news with
shocked amazement on their faces. Jane Crow
caught cheating? It didn't seem possible.

'Someone saw her,' Jack Gilbert was saying. 'But
they're not saying who.'

The students were huddled round the radiator in

the corridor on another freezing day. The windows were steamed up and the fog made the atmosphere oppressive.

'What's going on?' asked Lucy, nervously.

'It's Jane Crow. She cheated in yesterday's exam.' Jack sounded as if he could hardly believe what he had just said.

'Jane?' Lucy repeated. 'I don't believe it. She's completely straight.' Although Lucy usually felt she was an outsider, now she found herself one of the crowd. A feeling of importance, of acting on a stage to a huge audience overcame her, and then she felt ashamed.

'She isn't now,' said Sonia Tapping with faint malice.

'She's been suspended,' said Graham Browning.

'I don't believe this.' Lucy was determined to openly support Jane.

'Only for a day. But she's been disqualified from the exam as well.'

'We don't know who reported her,' continued Graham. 'It's being kept a secret – even from Jane.'

Sonia glanced at Lucy. 'Do *you* know who could have grassed on her?'

She shook her head firmly, fear clawing inside.

'No one seems to have the slightest clue,'

said Graham impatiently.

'But it must be someone who *saw* her cheat. Someone who was in the exam,' said Sonia. 'That narrows things down.'

'There must have been a mistake,' Lucy concluded. 'Jane would never cheat at anything.' She was beginning to feel sick with guilt.

Just then Jane's friends, Dawn and Sue, came up, arm in arm. Were they going to condemn Jane too, she wondered.

'Your best mate's been on the fiddle,' said Sonia. 'What do you reckon on that then?'

Dawn and Sue were just as attractive as Jane in their different ways. Dawn had long dark hair and huge, soulful eyes, and Sue was very tall with a commanding air. Lucy had always regarded them as nasty bits of work, with their vindictive and spiteful behaviour. She also thought they were both vain and rather stupid. Not in the same league as Jane at all.

But their response surprised Lucy. In fact, Dawn and Sue surprised them all.

'Jane's been ill,' said Sue. 'She got into a panic.'

'Jane would never have cheated if she hadn't been away for so long,' snapped Dawn. 'We're still her friends.' She looked round accusingly. 'We're going to stick by her.'

Lucy walked home slowly, pleased that she had supported Jane, but threatened by Dawn and Sue's unwelcome loyalty. Lucy had hoped they would condemn Jane, not want to see her again. Jane might come back to her then.

A frost was already settling and there was black ice on the road. Lucy had never felt so cold in her life and the November darkness had an icy grip. Suddenly she was seized with fear. Suppose someone found out that she had told on Jane? What would they all think? Would they reckon she had done her duty, or would they think she had been rotten to grass on Jane? Desperately, Lucy tried to reason with herself. Surely no one would have expected her to keep quiet. After all, cheating wasn't fair on anyone. But it was no good. Lucy knew all too clearly that although she had acted on impulse, she had told on Jane for the most selfish possible motives.

As she carefully made her way home along the icy pavements to her comfortably large and well-appointed house in Laurel Avenue, Lucy began to consider the extent of Jane's suffering. What must she be feeling now? What had she told her mother? Jane's parents were divorced and she lived alone with her mother who worshipped her daughter and was always bursting with pride over her achievements. Now Mrs Crow would be devastated.

Lucy's mother worked as a volunteer in the charity shop where Mrs Crow was manageress. She didn't need the money but wanted to be useful. Mrs Crow needed every penny. Despite their very different backgrounds, the two women had become friendly and Lucy knew her mother was bound to be full of Jane's disgrace when she got home.

Sleet began to fall and the sky above her was as dark and as threatening as her own conscience.

Lucy stepped out into the road, hardly conscious of what she was doing, her mind was so preoccupied. The car was upon her in a moment, roaring out of the twilight, hooting and only just avoiding her. Then the vehicle, its headlights blazing, was lost in the darkness.

Lucy shot back on to the pavement, shivering, so shocked she could hardly move. Then, with a tremendous mental effort, she forced herself to look right, left and right again, before darting across the dark and slippery road, arriving gasping on the other side.

Ten minutes later, Lucy sat at the kitchen table, still shaken, hoping her mother hadn't noticed how pale and shocked she looked. The house was quiet and warm in its spacious luxury. A clock chimed the half-hour and the large TV set glowed and muttered.

As her mother poured out strong tea, she began to describe how distraught Mrs Crow had been in the shop that morning.

'I've never seen her so upset.'

'Jane cheated in an exam,' Lucy said abruptly. Ironically, as she said the words, she could hear herself defending Jane to Jack and Sonia and Graham. *There must have been a mistake. Jane would never cheat at anything.* Then she heard Dawn saying, *We're still her friends. We're going to stand by her.* 'It was wrong,' Lucy added uneasily.

'Her mother's devastated. She never thought she would do such a thing. Of course, Maggie told me in confidence, but I expect it's all over town by now.'

'It's certainly all over school,' said Lucy, trying to stop herself from visibly shaking. She could still hear the car hooting and roaring towards her, its dazzling headlights blazing.

'Well, they're not going to be able to stop people gossiping, are they? The trouble is that Maggie was so proud of Jane and now she's so ashamed.'

Lucy fidgeted uneasily. The way her mother was talking made Jane's plight seem much worse.

'Apparently Jane was too ill to revise and she was so scared she was going to fail that she wrote out as much information as she could on her arm for that history exam. Then someone saw Jane cheating and reported her. It wasn't a very nice thing to do...' Mrs Brent's voice trailed away.

Lucy felt a wave of panic. She had thought her mother would condemn Jane, not feel sorry for her. If only she could own up, get her to understand why she had decided to go to Mrs Greenway. But how could she possibly confide now?

'It's not fair that Jane cheated,' Lucy said awkwardly. 'No one else did.'

'I'm not defending her,' said Mrs Brent. 'Obviously cheating's wrong. But I'm sure she's not the only one. That school has a very mixed bag of students.'

Lucy sighed. Her mother had always been a bit of a snob as far as Lady Thornton was concerned.

She would have preferred Lucy to have gone to the grammar school, but she simply hadn't been clever enough.

'If someone saw Jane cheating, they were duty-bound to report her,' Lucy continued firmly, desperately seeking justification, trying to convince herself more than anything. 'Surely you can see that, Mum? Why should she get good results on the fiddle?'

'Of course she shouldn't. But I know Mrs Crow. This will be a terrible blow to her when she thought Jane was getting on so well. All this is bound to go against her.'

'What's that got to do with it?' demanded Lucy angrily. 'Jane still cheated, Mum. There can't be one law for people who have bad luck and another for those who don't –'

Mrs Brent sighed. 'I'm sure you're right, dear. But whoever *did* tell… Well –' She paused. 'I just wouldn't like to have the Crow family on *my* conscience.'

Her mother's words hung between them and Lucy felt another twinge of panic. She had almost convinced herself that she had gone to Mrs Greenway for the right motives when deep down she knew that she hadn't at all.

For a moment she again considered confessing to her mother. But she knew she couldn't, and it was no use talking to Dad. He was a high-powered businessman and rarely at home, and anyway he wouldn't want to know. Lucy felt confused and unsure of herself. It was as if she had suddenly become a number of different people. One Lucy had told Mrs Greenway about Jane's cheating. Another had proclaimed Jane's innocence to her fellow students. And yet another Lucy had condemned her to her mother.

'Oh, by the way,' Mrs Brent said, taking a cottage pie out of the oven. 'You've got a letter. Someone dropped it in by hand. It was too dark to see who it was.' She smiled. 'Maybe they counted on that. Could it be from Chris?' She paused, looking at Lucy hopefully. 'I thought I heard something, but when I opened the door all I could see was a fish and chip van driving away.'

Mrs Brent was always worrying about her daughter's limited social life. Since leaving primary school she seemed to go out less and less. But last week, at a rare party, Lucy had briefly danced with a boy called Chris who was in the year above her at school. He had soon drifted off, but Lucy had falsely claimed he had spent longer with her than he had. Mrs Brent had been delighted and had gone on about Chris obsessively – much to Lucy's annoyance.

'Chris?' she asked in surprise and her mother frowned.

'You're an attractive and intelligent girl,' she snapped. 'Don't be so surprised that a boy wants to write you a letter.'

Lucy went out to the hall table and picked up an envelope which had her name and address written in childish-looking capital letters on the front. That's a bit odd, she thought, as she stuffed it into her pocket and made her way upstairs to change out of her school uniform before tea.

Mrs Brent watched her daughter's retreating back with annoyance, wishing that she would confide and feeling frustrated that she never did.

Lucy opened the envelope in the privacy of her bedroom. Inside was a card and for a moment she wondered if it was another invitation to a party. Although she was nervous about going to them, she often dreamed about meeting someone who led her into a whirlwind romance. But meeting Chris hadn't been much of a whirlwind or a romance. He had never spoken to her again.

'I think you need a change of hairstyle,' Mum had told her last week. 'Now that would give you a bit more confidence. Why don't you let me book you into Anton's?'

Lucy had refused point blank. She hated her mother interfering in her life and was determined to resist, even though she knew it was to her own disadvantage.

Lucy turned the card over curiously, trying to feel hopeful.

Then she froze, and a jolt of terror filled her as she caught sight of the front.

Stuck to the card was a cut-out engraving of a tall, thin man in a dark cloak, his face dour and expressionless, a scythe slung over his shoulder. Lucy knew who he was at once. The Angel of Death, the Grim Reaper.

She held her breath as she opened the home-made card. Scrawled inside were the words HAPPY DEATH DAY.

Lucy's hands began to shake and a sick feeling rose up into her throat. Who could have sent such a horrible message? It had to be someone with a very warped sense of humour. Or was it someone who was seriously disturbed?

She had always enjoyed scary things, even horror videos. She was often bored without a best friend to do things with and liked to have a feeling of safe fear in the comfort of her home, knowing the TV horror was cosily frightening, unlike real life which was raw, unfair and lonely. But the card had penetrated her like a blast of freezing cold air. Again, Lucy heard the sudden sound of the car's brakes screaming as she stepped off the pavement. She had just escaped death that very afternoon. Had that been a warning? Was she going to be punished for the terrible thing she had done?

3

I was right, school was awful, but what happened afterwards was even worse. Firstly I nearly got run over on the way home, and now someone's sent me a Happy Death Day card. I feel as if I'm going to pass out. My heart's racing and I'm trembling all over. Who would play such a horrible joke? I've just got to remember that it is a joke. And I've got to try and act normal around Mum. I don't need her interfering. But it's hard. I keep feeling as if I'm being watched. But by who? Maybe I'm just imagining it. After all, I've had a nasty shock...

Writing the events in her diary made Lucy feel slightly better, although a cold feeling in the pit of her stomach remained. Maybe she was taking the card too seriously. Surely it was just a joke?

'Lucy?' shouted her mother from downstairs. 'What are you doing up there?'

'I'm going to have a bath,' she yelled back.

'Not now. I've got your tea ready.'

Lucy groaned. All this anxiety and Mum too.

She got up and went to the window, pulling down the sash, desperate for fresh air, however cold. Her bedroom had suddenly become incredibly hot and she felt as if she was suffocating.

The freezing air was bitter and carried the smell of fog and frost, but Lucy stood there, breathing it in gratefully. Behind the quiet avenue of large gabled houses was a densely wooded hill. The moon had broken through the clouds, lighting a path through the trees with milky white light.

As Lucy gazed out at the wood, a tall thin man in a dark flowing coat suddenly appeared, walking slowly down the pale path, a bulky object slung over his shoulder.

He paused and seemed to be staring right up at her, his head thrown back. Then he began to walk a little faster, until he reached the junction with the road and came to a halt underneath the yellow beam of a street light. He was tall and scruffy-looking with a long narrow unshaven face. His coat was torn and ragged. Seconds later, he took off again down the avenue, gazing at the names of the houses until he reached Lucy's front gate. He rested a talon-like hand on it for a moment, staring down and nodding as if reassured. Then he turned and began to stumble down the road as if he was exhausted. At the bottom the man stopped and looked back.

Horrified, Lucy found she was gazing straight into his deep–set eyes.

Then he was off again, his coat flowing around him, almost as if he was wearing a swirling cloak. Lucy watched as he adjusted the object on his back with some effort, as if whatever he was carrying was heavy and cumbersome, and his coat swirled again in a breeze that didn't exist.

Lucy shuddered. He looked exactly like the figure on the card. The card that *must* be a joke. A sick joke. Then the man disappeared round the corner and she heard a blast of heavy rock music from the open window of a car. Lucy recognised the driver as Greg Smith, a neighbouring teenager. Had he noticed the man in his tattered overcoat, or was he invisible to everyone but her?

'Lucy!' Her mother was getting annoyed now. 'What on earth do you think you're doing?'

'Who sent that letter?' asked Mrs Brent over supper.

'It was an invitation,' lied Lucy as she ate her portion of cottage pie. She felt confused and apprehensive.

'Who from?'

'A boy at school – for a disco next month.'

'That's a long way ahead.' Her mother gave Lucy a satisfied smile. 'He *must* be anxious to book you up. This wouldn't be the famous Chris, would it?'

Lucy nodded. To lie was possible; to confide was not.

That night Lucy slept lightly, tossing and turning, worrying herself into such a frantic state that she began to dream.

Lucy was walking in the hillside woods on a warm spring day and the leaves on the trees, fresh and green, were rustling in a light wind. She began to run, following a winding woodland path that she had known all her life, until she came to a small valley, packed with bluebells.

Slowing down, Lucy began to pick her way through the carpet of flowers towards an ivy-covered mound at the head of the valley. Ripping away the thick leafy stems, she soon saw she had uncovered a gravestone, and the black lettering leapt out at her from the veined marble surface.

**RIP
LUCY BRENT
HAPPY BIRTHDAY**

Lucy woke sweating, gasping for air, deeply afraid but unable to remember what her nightmare had been about. Then the dreadful images returned and she sat up in bed, clasping her head.

Happy Death Day read the card that she had thrown under the bed last night. Lucy leant over and to her horror found that it was still there. For a moment she had hoped the card was part of her nightmare. But it wasn't. And her birthday was only three days away. What was she going to do? Who could she tell? But Lucy knew there was no one she could confide in. No one at all.

wednesday, 9th

I feel terrified and exhausted this morning and my head's swimming with horrifying images. Last night, in my dream, I saw my own grave...what does that mean? Could it be linked to the card? Who could have sent it to me? Is it just a joke, or is someone really stalking me? Suppose I am going to die. I'm too scared to write any more – I don't want to think about it...

As she dressed, Lucy had a sudden idea. Suppose Jane had managed to find out that she had betrayed her? Would *she* have sent her the card? If she had Lucy would be very relieved, for that at least meant some marauding stranger wasn't watching her. Then she remembered the dark man outside. He looked like a vagrant, a tramp. But Lucy had never seen any vagrants in this affluent area of town. Where had he come from?

Lucy went to the window and looked out, only to find that there was a light scattering of snow. She could see a set of footprints leading up the path through the woods and shivered, her stomach churning as she remembered the grave she had uncovered in her dream. Her own grave.

RIP
LUCY BRENT
HAPPY BIRTHDAY

The thought of the grave sent Lucy into a blind panic and she was so afraid that she could barely bring herself to move. An accident might happen to her at any moment, making the terrible prediction come true.

'What are you doing, Lucy?' shouted her mother up the stairs. 'You're going to be late for school.'

'I'm coming,' she stammered. 'I'm coming, Mum.' But she still stood rooted to the spot, now convinced that if she moved she might fall down the stairs and break her neck. But then the ceiling could also fall in or a plane might crash on to the house. She was doomed.

'Lucy?' Her mother's voice was even louder and sounded alarmed.

Lucy opened her bedroom door, and forcing herself to put one foot in front of the other she slowly edged her way along the landing. But when she reached the head of the stairs she froze again, gazing down in horror, unable to believe how steep the descent was.

Sure that she would never reach the bottom without falling, Lucy swayed slightly, gripping the hand-rail which felt as if it might break away at any moment. Slowly, she began to edge her way down, an acute feeling of vertigo almost overpowering her, the stairs seeming to shimmer strangely, unsteadying her even more.

Halfway down she stopped, one hand still gripping the flimsy rail, knowing she couldn't continue, worrying that her mother would come out of the kitchen and think she was ill. Dad had already left the house. He got up at six and was never home before nine. Sometimes it seemed as if he hardly existed.

Lucy stared down hopelessly at the shimmering drop and realised she would have to go down backwards, on all fours. Turning round, she began to crawl, at last feeling safer.

With a huge sense of relief, she reached the bottom and hurried into the downstairs toilet, sweating, suddenly realising the day stretched before her like a minefield.

4

'What on earth kept you?'

Lucy so wanted to tell her mother, to be comforted by her, but she bit back the words before they came out when she saw how furious her mother was.

Lucy wondered if her anger had anything to do with Dad. She was sure her parents' relationship was getting worse, and she wondered if it was the reason for her father's even longer absences from home.

'I had a bad dream,' she muttered.

'Why was that?' her mother asked brusquely.

'I don't know.'

'You're not worrying about anything?' She was slightly warmer now.

'No.'

Afraid of choking to death, Lucy ate her breakfast slowly, chewing each mouthful carefully, reducing each bite to the smallest possible morsel.

Several times her mother looked at her daughter oddly, but didn't say anything. Eventually, however, she couldn't contain herself any longer.

'You're going to be late,' she snapped. 'Try and eat up.'

Lucy rose to her feet, leaving the rest of her toast. 'I'll go now.'

'You've still got time to finish your breakfast,' said Mrs Brent in mounting agitation. 'Don't get so worked up.'

'You told me to hurry – and anyway, it's snowing. I ought to allow some extra time.'

Mrs Brent sighed, as if there was little point in trying to communicate any further. 'Off you go then!' she said briskly.

Lucy knew she was behaving in the most ridiculous way, but the horror of the card and the dream wouldn't go away. She stepped carefully down the snow-bound winter garden path, desperately anxious not to slip. Then, having survived that ordeal, she checked the road was clear so many times she began to feel dizzy.

This has got to stop, Lucy told herself, but she was feeling increasingly out of control.

Happy Death Day. The words on the card became a chant in her mind that wouldn't go away. *Happy Death Day. Happy…*

The snow was falling gently, and Lucy was

terrified of slipping over. All she had to do was fall and break her leg which would then become septic, turn to gangrene and have to be amputated. Then the infection would spread – and she would die in agony.

Lucy was so preoccupied that she didn't see Jane at the school gates until it was too late. She was alone and her face was parchment grey. Lucy was so flustered she gave Jane a too-cheerful 'Hello!' Worse still, she followed this by clumsily blurting out, 'I'm so sorry about the trouble.'

Jane walked on without speaking, while Lucy followed, jabbering at her.

'I'm really sorry. I know how ill you've been. I just wanted to say I understand and would never hold it –'

Slowly Jane turned round to stare at Lucy blankly, as if she hardly existed. 'Why don't you just push off?' she said contemptuously and hurried away.

As Lucy sat at her desk waiting for the lesson to begin, she listened miserably to the idle chatter. 'I just couldn't believe she'd do such a thing,' said Caroline Blake.

Jane had not yet arrived, and there was a buzz of anticipation.

How long would she have to go on suffering, wondered Lucy, realising that Jane had been reduced to a scapegoat, and everyone was off-loading their bad feelings on to her – and enjoying doing so.

Caroline Blake stared ahead. 'It's not fair on the rest of us,' she said reflectively.

There was a sudden hush as Jane arrived in the classroom, walking slowly and casually to her place between Sue and Dawn. They both grinned supportively at her. It was as if they were Jane's handmaidens. But everyone else looked hostile, except Lucy who had hoped she might exchange a friendly glance with Jane. But there seemed no chance of that.

Jane sat down and opened her bag, yawned slightly, and pulled out her homework book. The silence deepened, broken only by the odd, subdued cough.

Everyone's eyes were on Jane as she turned round and glanced at the class disdainfully. It was a studied performance but highly effective, and Lucy felt a grudging admiration. Her cool gaze continued to dominate them, making everyone feel uncomfortable – except Dawn and Sue.

As Lucy watched, her thoughts returned to the card. Had Jane sent it? It would be a relief if she had, even if it meant that Jane knew she had told on her. But suppose she *hadn't* sent her the card? Suppose it had been sent by a wandering maniac like the vagrant who had walked so menacingly out of the woods? She just couldn't get the repetitive thoughts out of her mind.

As she sat deep in thought, Mrs Granger arrived to take the English lesson and the tension heightened like an overstretched elastic band.

5

The snow had stopped falling by break-time, but although there was still only a light covering, the surface of the playground was slippery. An icy wind had sprung up and now she was outside Lucy found the conditions even more menacing than she had thought they would be.

The class waited, shivering, for their Games teacher. Only Jane seemed composed, doing some warm-up exercises against the wall. When Mrs Beacon arrived, Lucy was ready for her.

'I'm afraid I can't do Games,' she said awkwardly.

'Have you got a note?' asked Mrs Beacon irritably.

'No.'

'Then you'll have to –'

'I slipped in the snow on the way to school and turned my ankle. It's very painful.' Turned seemed the right kind of phrase. Sprained would have been too dramatic, particularly as her ankle wasn't in the least swollen.

'Have you seen the nurse?'

'Not yet.'

'Then go and see her. *Now*, Lucy.'

*

'I honestly can't find anything wrong,' said Mrs James, the school nurse. 'But I must say you do look peaky, so I should give Games a miss today. Go and tell Mrs Beacon what I said.'

Lucy put on her coat with relief, but as she returned to the playground she slipped and almost fell. She stood stock still, shivering with fright, unable to move because she was sure she would fall again. Desperately she tried to force herself onwards but it was no good, her legs wouldn't budge.

Eventually, the bell went and the netball game came to a sudden halt at Mrs Beacon's final whistle. The class came racing towards Lucy, headed by Jane, closely followed by Sue and Dawn, Unaware that Lucy was stranded, they ran past her and she felt invisible.

Shortly afterwards Mrs Beacon arrived, the ball under her arm.

'What on earth are you doing, Lucy?' she demanded.

'I'm frightened to move.'

'In case you "turn" your ankle?' Mrs Beacon asked sarcastically.

'In case I slip.'

'Don't be ridiculous.'

'I mean it.'

'So you propose to stay there until the snow melts?'

'Please help me.' She was close to tears now.

'Is someone bullying you?' Mrs Beacon rapped out. 'Has someone *told* you to stand in the middle of the playground without moving?'

'No.'

'Then why are you being so stupid?' Mrs Beacon was fast running out of patience.

'I'm not. I can't move.' Lucy was beginning to cry now. 'I can't move in case I slip.'

With a sigh Mrs Beacon grabbed her arm and together they walked slowly off the snow and ice on to a gravel path that had been cleared by the caretaker.

'Do you feel safe now, Lucy?' she asked more gently.

'Yes.'

'And you're sure you're not being bullied?'

'No.'

Mrs Beacon sighed again. 'If you change your mind and want to talk, you know where to find me.'

Lucy nodded and Mrs Beacon hurried away, looking perplexed.

During the rest of the day Lucy occasionally glimpsed Jane, self-contained, face expressionless, waited upon by Dawn and Sue, deserted by the rest of her friends. Several times, Lucy almost plucked up enough courage to confess to what she had done, and to ask Jane if she had sent her the card, but her aloof self-containment made it impossible.

When she wasn't thinking about Jane, Lucy's thoughts turned to the vagrant walking down the hill in the moonlight, and the strange object he'd been carrying that she didn't dare to think about. Sitting miserably in the art class, Lucy absent-mindedly drew him rather than the vase with a poppy design that sat on the table in front of the class. As she drew, a name for the vagrant suddenly appeared in her mind. The Dark Man. She shivered.

Lucy drew the Dark Man carefully in pen and ink as, tall and gaunt and vengeful, he strode down threateningly from the woods. Would she see him tonight, she wondered, the dread stirring in her as she remembered how he had looked at the number on her gate so carefully. Please God, don't let anything happen to me. Her birthday was now two days away. Was that going to be her death day?

And was the Dark Man really the Grim Reaper?

As her thoughts became unbearable, Lucy tried to rationalise the situation.

Suppose Jane *had* sent her the card? Was she just winding her up because she had guessed, or somehow found out what she had done? If so, wasn't the card a bit subtle? Surely Jane would have been much more angry with her than that. Why hadn't she confronted her, rather than just sending a silly card?

But what if someone else had sent her the card? Someone who wasn't normal? Was the Dark Man normal? He certainly didn't look it. But supposing it was him, what was his motive? Uncomfortable thoughts began churning inside Lucy's head, the underlying guilt making her imagination all the sharper.

'That's a funny looking vase,' said Miss Daniels, the art teacher, looking over Lucy's shoulder.

'Sorry, miss. I was doodling.'

'Who is he?'

'Someone I saw –'

'He certainly looks sinister.' Miss Daniels's voice carried across the classroom and Jane glanced round. Was she smiling, or had a shadow stolen over her face? It was hard to tell. 'And what's that he's carrying?' she asked curiously.

'I think it's a scythe, miss.'

'You don't know? After all – you're the artist.'

Most of the class were giggling now, and Jane glanced round again.

'A scythe? A tall man with a scythe?' Miss Daniels was enjoying the joke. 'Why, I do believe you've drawn the Grim Reaper himself.'

'Who, miss?' asked Lucy feebly.

'The Grim Reaper. The mythical figure who comes to claim the souls of the dead.' The giggling broke out again, but it was quickly silenced by Miss Daniels. 'I've never seen you draw so well, Lucy,' she said, smiling, 'and I mean that.'

'I'd –' Lucy was completely at a loss for words.

'It's a really imaginative piece of work.'

'I'll draw the vase,' whispered Lucy. 'I'm sorry.'

'I'll take your Grim Reaper and put him up on the wall. Maybe your confidence will improve if you see him there every day.' Miss Daniels took the drawing and pinned it up.

Although Jane had her back to her now, Lucy was certain she was smiling.

The winter darkness closed in as Lucy walked slowly and carefully home, avoiding the icy patches, dodging pedestrians who seemed to be literally hurtling along the pavements. But the worst was still to come – she still had to cross the road. She waited for a long time at the kerb, too scared to cross because the traffic was roaring past, black and monstrous, lethal with blazing headlights.

Several people glanced at her curiously as they hurried across the road. But no one offered to help.

As she stood indecisively, the noise of the rush-hour traffic seemed to grow even louder and Lucy knew that she daren't cross until the road was completely clear.

'Lucy?'

Mrs Beacon was suddenly beside her, looking anxious. In one way Lucy was pleased to see her for she knew she would help her. In another, she was deeply embarrassed – first the incident in the playground and now this.

'What's the matter?'

'I'm scared to cross.'

'What's the problem? Most of the ice has melted.'

'There's too much traffic.'

Mrs Beacon gazed down at her in alarm. 'But you come home this way every day.'

'I know.'

'You can't be this scared every time.'

'I'm not.'

'So what's the problem?'

'I don't know.'

'Are you telling me the truth?'

'I'm trying to.'

'What's that supposed to mean?' Mrs Beacon was uneasy now.

'There's too much traffic,' she repeated doggedly.

'OK, I'll take you across, but you've *got* to tell me what you're *really* frightened about.'

'Getting killed.' There – it was out and Lucy felt a great rush of relief. She had told someone at last.

'*What?*'

'Getting killed,' she repeated.

'You mean – run over?'

'I mean getting killed – somehow – anyhow.'

Mrs Beacon gave Lucy a strange look and then, taking her arm, helped her across the road, guiding her briskly but reassuringly.

When they reached the other side, Mrs Beacon said, 'Why don't you tell me what's really bothering you. Is there anything wrong at home?'

'Nothing.'

'Or at school?'

Lucy shook her head.

'Where do you live?'

'Laurel Avenue.'

'That's not far from here. Shall I walk you back?'

Lucy gazed up at Mrs Beacon, recognising her kindness and her strong desire to help. But, just like her parents, she knew Mrs Beacon would think her crazy if she told her the Dark Man – the Grim Reaper – was sizing her up.

'I'm really fine now. Thanks all the same.'

Mrs Beacon, however, wasn't prepared to give up so easily. 'Look, Lucy, There *is* something wrong and we need to talk about it. Come and see me at school tomorrow and we can have a chat.'

Lucy nodded, making a mental note to keep out of her way.

What a fool I've made of myself - Mrs Beacon is going to think I'm nuts. First she had to help me off the icy playground, and then she had to

guide me across the road – a road I've crossed a
hundred times before. But I had to take care –
I could easily have had a lethal accident in all
that slippery ice and snow. I feel a bit better
now that I'm home, but I'm sure yesterday's
brush with a car was a warning...a hint of things
to come. If I close my eyes, I can hear the
screeching of brakes, see myself falling under
the wheels, feel the agonising pain. I need a
friend more than ever now, someone I can talk
to – if only I could talk to Jane.

Lucy was exhausted by supper-time and hardly ate
a thing. Her mother had decided to take much the
same questioning approach as Mrs Beacon, which
was incredibly annoying, but Lucy was trapped at
the table and she knew she had to respond
somehow.

'I'm sure there's something wrong,' Mrs Brent
was saying. 'All that slowness this morning, and
now you won't eat. I'd better take your
temperature.'

Lucy sighed heavily, wishing her mother wasn't
such a fusspot. But then a thought struck her. If she
could convince her mother that she was ill and

should stay at home, she would not only avoid the possibility of something happening to her, but she would also be able to avoid Jane and Mrs Beacon as well. The more she thought about the idea, the more attractive it seemed.

'I *am* feeling a bit off colour, Mum,' Lucy began tentatively.

'What sort of off colour?'

'A bit sick. Slightly giddy. I've felt that way all day.'

'I'll get the thermometer.'

'I haven't got a temperature.'

'Let's just see, shall we?'

Mrs Brent got her first aid box out of a cupboard and produced the thermometer with a look of triumph in her eyes.

As Lucy expected, her temperature was normal, but this didn't seem to deter her mother at all.

'Well you must have caught a chill, love. Why don't you go upstairs to bed and I'll bring up a hot-water bottle and a milky drink. Soon have you right as rain. It's your birthday the day after tomorrow. You'll be a teenager! You don't want to be ill on your birthday, do you? Especially as it's the day of the theatre trip.'

In all the horror of what had been happening,

Lucy had completely forgotten about that – and now the whole idea seemed like just another hazard.

Lucy looked down at her bed in the cosy glow of her bedside lamp. The pillow, decorated with lambs skipping across an idyllic meadow that she had had since she was a baby, looked particularly inviting. Surely nothing could happen to her if she stayed in bed? Then she realised with a kind of hollow misery that she could dream, and the ivy-covered grave floated menacingly into her mind.

Lucy went to the window and gazed out, fearful that she would see the Dark Man again. The moon seemed even brighter tonight, picking out every shadow on the wooded hill, but there was no sign of anyone about.

Suddenly she felt safer. The Dark Man wasn't coming. Maybe she would never see him again.

Lucy gave a sigh of relief, but as she stole a final glance at the wood, she choked back a scream – a shadow was moving on the hill.

Lucy was hardly able to breathe. In the bright moonlight she could see him with a clarity that was terrifying. And she was sure the Dark Man was looking up at her window, trying to catch her eye. He walked slowly but relentlessly down the hill, his steps dragging, heading for her front gate.

'Lucy!'

She wheeled round, not having heard her mother come into the room.

'What are you doing? You'll catch your death,' she pronounced as she put down the tray with its milky drink on the bedside table.

Lucy glanced back out of the window again and literally shook with fear, her jaw locked, teeth clenched. The Dark Man was at the gate. He had his hand on the latch.

Lucy screamed. 'There's a man out there,' she sobbed.

Mrs Brent hurried over to the window, blocking the view. 'There's no one there, darling,' she said quietly. 'No one I can see.'

'There *was* a man there,' Lucy repeated. 'Leaning on the gatepost. He was trying to get in.'

'Nonsense. There's no one there at all. Come and have another look with me.' Mrs Brent gently pulled her shivering daughter back to the window. 'You see?'

She was right. The avenue was empty.

'I'm sorry,' Lucy blurted out. 'I must have been

mistaken.' But she was sure she hadn't been.

'You've got yourself into a nervy state. Now get straight into bed and I'll make sure the bedbugs don't bite.' This was one of her mother's favourite phrases and now it seemed particularly comforting. 'The bolt's on the front door and your dad's home early.'

Lucy thought the first of the two statements was the most reassuring. She had never really thought of her father as protecting her for he was too remote, and if he really *had* come home early she was sure there would be a row.

Lucy thought again of the Dark Man with his hand resting on the garden gate, the curved thing on his back, and the raw fear abruptly returned.

7

My imagination is getting the better of me -
I've got to pull myself together. The Dark Man
is just another vagrant, an old tramp who lives
out on the hill. And I'm just frightening myself
into being frightened. THERE'S NO GRIM REAPER
OUT THERE. THAT'S ONLY SOME POOR HOMELESS
MAN. As for the card, I'm sure it was Jane who
sent it, and if she sends more I can deal with
it. After all it's just a stupid card. If I'm
honest, I deserved it.

I'm going to bed and I'm going to sleep, and
I'm not going to have any more horrible dreams...

Lucy drifted off into an uneasy sleep, but was
abruptly woken by a shouting voice and the
certainty that the Dark Man had got into the
house.

She sat up in bed and listened fearfully until she
realised the shouting voice belonged to her father.

She got out of bed, pulled open her door and
stood at the top of the stairs. Her parents often had

rows, but this sounded like a particularly bad one. She could hear angry, bitter voices.

Lucy went back into her room and quietly closed her door.

She got into bed and tried to shut out the shouting, but it seemed to penetrate her very soul. How did her parents keep going with all this quarrelling, Lucy wondered. She felt caught up in their web of misery and, not for the first time, wondered if their misery was her fault, that in some way she had failed them.

Lucy felt her parents' arguments were sapping her strength, making her less and less of a person. Soon she would be a mere shadow, no match for the Dark Man as he walked down the hill to warn her that her life would soon be at an end. She shivered at the gruesome picture in her head. When would he finally come to fetch her? she wondered.

As these desperate thoughts hammered in her head, Lucy realised her heart was beating far too fast, much faster than ever before, pounding, making so much noise that her bedroom became one big heartbeat. Again and again she closed her eyes against the thumping sound, frantically trying to regulate it, and then suddenly it went to the other extreme, slowing right down and becoming a single beat with irregular pauses, like an ancient clock that might stop at any moment.

She sat up in bed, terrified. What was happening to her? Was she having a heart attack? The beat became fast again, so fast that she was gasping for air, and then minutes later, it returned to being ponderously slow. Soon it was so erratic that she lay back in terror, not wanting to disturb her parents' argument, but so frightened the sweat was streaming down her brow, soaking the sheets as if she had a fever.

After what seemed like hours, her heartbeat finally steadied, and her exhausted mind slipped into sleep again. She found herself following a path through the woods, hand-in-hand with the Dark Man whose grip was icy cold. They walked silently through a tunnel of trees, and in the distance she could see a patch of thick undergrowth. When they reached the tangle of foliage, the Dark Man parted the bushes and Lucy found herself staring at her own grave, festooned in ivy that rustled in a chilly wind. It was too cold to snow, but there was a thick coating underfoot and Lucy's toes were numb.

Slowly, the ivy began to peel away and the grave

opened to reveal a simple pine coffin. The Dark Man began to lead Lucy towards what she thought was her final resting place, his grip as icy as before, and when she looked down again the coffin was open.

Suddenly the Dark Man changed shape and became her father, dropping a red rose into the grave. Lucy peered into the open coffin, and saw her mother, white and waxy in her shroud. Her father began to sing in a clear, pure baritone: 'O my love is like a red, red rose, That's newly sprung in June.'

'No!' shouted Lucy. 'She can't be *dead*. Mum loves me. She loves us both.'

But her father only repeated the lines of the song, his voice crystal clear in the snow-bound woods, the words wounding Lucy like shards of glass.

Lucy woke with a gasp, scrambling to her feet, disentangling herself from the shroud-like bedclothes. That had been the worst dream yet. Too afraid to go back to sleep, and desperate for it to be morning, she drew back the curtains. Snowflakes were falling steadily, softly, suffocatingly on the grass outside.

8

Thursday, 10th

So much for not having any horrible dreams —
that was the worst yet. It's 6.00am and I
can't get back to sleep. Most dreams I forget in
a few seconds, but I can't get this one out of
my mind. And I can't stop thinking about my
birthday tomorrow — will it be my Death Day
too? I can't face the thought of going to school
— I'm terrified something will happen to me.

'I had a terrible dream,' Lucy told her mother when
she came up to her room with a cup of tea. 'I feel
awful.'

'You'd better not go to school, love. I want to see
you're better by your birthday. But I'll still have to
go in to work. There'll be no one to open the shop.
I'll only stay for a couple of hours. Mrs Crow will
be there by twelve.'

Her mother seemed flustered and there were
bags under her eyes. Lucy wondered how long the
row had lasted between her parents — and what

the consequences had been.

'And if you feel worse you can always phone me and I'll come home immediately, shop or no shop. I don't think you've got anything too bad though. Maybe you're just overtired.' Mrs Brent was talking very fast now, as if she didn't want Lucy to ask any questions.

'Mum –'

'Yes?' She looked at her daughter warily.

'What were you and Dad having a row about last night?'

'Did we keep you awake?'

'Not really, but –'

'I'm sorry.' Her mother frowned and then for once decided to come clean. 'It's the same old problem.'

'Dad never at home?'

'And when he is, he's too tired to talk. It just gets to me, that's all.'

'What about him?' asked Lucy.

'He can't seem to change.'

They gazed at each other in silence; there seemed nothing else to say.

'I won't be long,' said her mother, trying to be reassuring. 'If you feel bad, just ring the shop.'

*

Lucy lay in bed, listening to the creaks and rattles, shiftings and stirrings that were the inner life of the house.

Water pipes groaned, the washing machine rumbled as it began another cycle, the telephone rang and went on ringing for what seemed a long time before it stopped. Some late post slipped through the letterbox, landing with a soft thud on the hall carpet, a tap began to drip, the doorbell rang but didn't ring again, the central heating system gave an occasional clank, and a wind sprang up outside.

Lucy felt comforted by the familiar sounds, and was just drifting off to sleep when she heard tapping on her windowpane, and began to shake with fear. The tapping was at first sporadic, but soon became much more insistent. How could someone be knocking on her windowpane, so many metres above the ground? Then, sitting up in bed, Lucy saw the wisteria stems beating their insistent rhythm. She closed her eyes, exhausted and ashamed, starting when she heard the droning of a plane above, sure the aircraft was flying too low over the house. The drone became a scream and –

Lucy leapt out of bed, shaking. She couldn't bear

to stay there for another moment. She would get up and watch TV downstairs. As she dressed her head began to ache, and soon it was throbbing so viciously that she could hardly think straight. The doorbell began to ring again and she walked slowly and apprehensively to the window.

Peering out, Lucy could just make out a familiar figure and her heart began to pound again so painfully that she could hardly breathe.

The Dark Man stood by the front door, the curved object strapped across his shoulder. Had he come to claim her in daylight?

What was she going to do? Call the police? Could they protect her against the messenger of death?

Then the Dark Man began to walk away without looking back, staring straight ahead as he made off down the avenue. Lucy watched him until he was out of sight.

She didn't want to be alone any longer. Staying at home, thinking she might be safe there, had been a huge mistake, for Lucy had only opened herself up to even more danger. Glancing at her watch, she saw that it was only ten and her mother wouldn't be back for another two hours. What was she going to do?

Suddenly, she decided to phone Mrs Jakes, her next door neighbour, a kind but over-talkative woman who had four children and a husband who was a truck driver. Bert Jakes had worked hard and had made a good deal of money, and the family had moved into the avenue a couple of years ago, much to Lucy's parents' barely concealed disapproval. In fact, this was about the only subject they ever agreed on. Mum described Mrs Jakes as 'mutton dressed as lamb', and she would occasionally add mysteriously that she wasn't 'as good as she should be'. Dad contented himself with saying, 'They bring the Laurels down. They're not right for the neighbourhood.'

It was true that their back garden was an untidy mess, and the front much the same, but unlike her own parents, Mr and Mrs Jakes radiated warmth and love. And there was something – someone – else. Flo. The Jakes' black cat. Lucy's parents had never wanted pets in the house but Lucy had befriended Flo who roamed the street outside. Flo would come up and rub herself against Lucy's legs. What's more, the black cat regularly got into Lucy's back garden and after she'd made a fuss of her, she would pick Flo up, and return her to Mrs Jakes. As a result, Mrs Jakes, Flo and Lucy had struck up quite a friendship.

Lucy hurried to the phone and dialled her neighbour's number, almost shouting aloud with joy when she got through.

'It's Lucy,' she stuttered.

'Hello, love. How are you?' Mrs Jakes sounded natural and ordinary and cheerful, the best antidote to the Dark Man she could possibly imagine.

'I'm not well.'

'I'm sorry to hear that,' said Mrs Jakes and Lucy was deeply touched by the concern in her voice.

'And I'm scared.'

'Scared? How's that?'

'There's this man. He kept ringing the bell.'

'Did he now.' She sounded fierce. 'I hope you didn't open the door.'

'No way.'

'Where is he now?'

'He walked away.'

'In what direction?'

'The town.'

'Funny I didn't see him. When was this?'

'A few minutes ago.'

'Well, that *is* odd. I've been cleaning the front

room all morning. I didn't see anyone.'

'Are you sure?'

'Absolutely. What did he look like?'

'Very tall and dark, unshaven, with a tatty old overcoat. He came down from the woods carrying something,' said Lucy, feeling scared all over again.

'Carrying what?'

'I'm not sure.'

'Your mum's at work?'

'She won't be back till twelve.'

'With you ill and –' Mrs Jakes broke off, realising she was bound to be seen as speaking out of turn. Quickly she changed tack. 'You're all alone in the house and scared out of your mind?'

'Yes,' Lucy admitted shakily.

'OK. I'll come over and look after you till Mum gets back.'

'Would you mind?'

'Not at all. I'd be glad to.' Mrs Jakes paused. 'You have got a telly, haven't you?'

When Mrs Jakes arrived she headed for a chair by the window, switched on the TV and sat down heavily. 'Mind if I watch my programme?'

'Go ahead,' said Lucy a little reluctantly. She'd hoped to have the chance to tell Mrs Jakes more about the Dark Man. But just to have her reassuringly common sense and ordinary presence in the house was such a bonus that nothing seemed to matter – even her mother's return. What on earth would Mum say when she discovered Mrs Jakes sitting in front of the TV? Lucy knew the answer. Her mother would be furious. But right now she didn't care.

Suddenly she heard a scratching sound outside the front door and Lucy felt the panic rising in her again.

'Oh dear,' said Mrs Jakes, getting up again. 'That'll be Flo. She wants to join us.' She smiled at Lucy.

'Let her in,' said Lucy recklessly.

'You're sure your mum won't mind?'

'I'm sure she won't.' I'm sure she will, Lucy thought uneasily.

Lucy returned to bed and fell asleep immediately, no longer afraid. With the reassuring presence of Mrs Jakes downstairs watching daytime TV with Flo on her lap, the house felt much safer.

She woke again at half-past eleven and went to her bedroom window, listening to the reassuringly lazy drone from the TV downstairs. The snow was falling gently, gradually reducing the wooded hill to a series of white humps and the footpath to a blurred outline.

Lucy shivered and looked away. She had never seen the hill look so cruel and bleak. Was there really an ivy-covered grave somewhere amongst the trees? She shivered again. Of course there wasn't. It was only in her guilty, confused mind.

She was about to pull the curtains against the sight when she caught a shadowy glimpse of someone walking up the avenue towards her, a blurred figure amongst the swirling snowflakes. Then she saw him. The Dark Man was stumbling past the house as if he was ill, gazing up at the hill. Then he started up the path, leaving footprints behind him, the bulky object still slung across his back.

Lucy tore herself away from the window, her heart hammering. Then she had a sudden thought. Had Mrs Jakes seen the Dark Man too?

Lucy wrenched open her bedroom door and headed for the stairs, but as she reached them something soft and furry ran between her legs, letting out a piercing miaow. A black cat. Suddenly

Lucy was falling into space, rolling over and over until she hit the hall floor with a loud, hard thump.

She sat up dazed, amazed that the accident she had been so much dreading had actually come at last and caused by a black cat which was surely meant to be magical. The Dark Man had passed by the house and with his passing had come her fall. Was she going to die? Had she just suffered some awful internal injury she wasn't feeling the effects of yet? Lucy waited for some tell-tale sign, surprised that she was not only still breathing but could only feel the odd bruise. From somewhere at the top of the stairs came a miaowing sound. It was only Flo, but was she acting as the Dark Man's emissary?

As Mrs Jakes came rushing out into the hall, Lucy waited for the real pain to come. The pain of death.

'Don't move, dear.' Mrs Jakes knelt down beside her, stroking her hair.

But Lucy was already pushing her aside and painfully rising to her feet, bruised and battered but amazingly unhurt. She looked back to the steep flight of stairs and saw a black tail disappearing round the corner.

'Are you all right?' Mrs Jakes was very upset.

'Just bruised. I tripped over the cat. It wasn't Flo's fault –' Lucy said hurriedly, although she had now convinced herself that Flo had deliberately tripped her.

'No. It was mine,' said Mrs Jakes. 'She just jumped off my lap and dashed upstairs. She must have thought she heard a mouse.'

'Mrs Jakes, did you see a man go past?'

'What kind of man?'

'Tall, dark, with something slung over his shoulder.'

'The one you saw before? No – I didn't see him.'

'You were sitting at the window all the time?'

'Yes.'

'You didn't move at all?'

'I was thinking of making some tea and bringing a cup up to you, but I didn't move – not until Flo jumped off my lap.'

Lucy calculated the chances of Mrs Jakes just missing the Dark Man. She supposed it was possible.

Then she heard the key turn in the front door.

'What's going on?' Mrs Brent looked dazed, staring at Mrs Jakes as if she could hardly believe she could be there. Then her surprise turned to anger.

'I just dropped in to keep an eye on Lucy.' Mrs Jakes sounded uneasy.

'You did what?' Mrs Brent was looking at her unexpected visitor in distaste, wrinkling her nose as if she smelt.

Mrs Jakes stumbled on unhappily. 'Unfortunately Lucy just tripped over my Flo –'

'Who?'

'My cat. She took a tumble down the stairs.'

'The cat?'

'No, Lucy.' Mrs Jakes was getting increasingly agitated.

'Are you all right?' Mrs Brent turned to her daughter in concern.

'I'm fine.' At least she thought she was. Unless there were hidden complications...

'Did you say cat?' Mrs Brent gazed at Mrs Jakes, at last beginning to understand.

'My Flo –'

'Where is she now?'

'She ran up the stairs. Naughty girl. That's how she tripped up Lucy.'

'Where is she *now*?' grated Mrs Brent.

'Still upstairs. I'll go and call her.' With some relief, Mrs Jakes hurried upstairs and they could hear her calling, 'Kitty, kitty, Flo? Kitty, kitty, Flo?

Come to Mumsie –'

Mrs Brent looked disgusted. 'How did that awful woman get in?'

Lucy was immediately indignant. 'She's *not* awful. She's kind. I asked her in.'

'But why?'

'I was scared.'

'What of?'

'I saw this man outside. He rang the bell. I didn't know what to do. You shouldn't have left me alone.'

'Lucy – I've got to work –'

'You don't have to go to that shop at all. You know it's only because you want to get out of the house.'

'So a man rang at the door? I expect he was trying to sell something.' Mrs Brent tried to be appeasing, but knew she stood no chance of success.

'I was scared. You shouldn't have left me alone,' Lucy repeated doggedly.

'So you asked that woman in?'

'Yes.'

'With her cat?'

'I like Flo.'

'She's probably ripping the place apart.'

'You shouldn't have done it, Mum,' Lucy insisted. 'You shouldn't have left me alone.'

'You're right, Lucy,' said Mrs Brent, suddenly repentant, despite the aggravation of Mrs Jakes's presence. 'I shouldn't have gone out and I'm sorry. The job keeps me sane. You go to school. Your father goes to work and I'm on my own here –' Mrs Brent tailed off, biting her trembling lower lip. Lucy put her arms around her forgivingly.

'I'm sorry too, Mum.'

'What about?'

'Being so stupid.'

'You weren't being stupid,' said Mrs Brent reassuringly. 'That man could have been anyone. I should have been here with you.'

Mrs Jakes could still be heard calling Flo on the landing. Then there was a scampering sound, the crash of breaking glass and a howl of anguish.

'That's my crystal bowl,' yelled Mrs Brent, pulling away from her daughter in mounting agitation.

'Naughty Flo!' Mrs Jakes sounded penitent and looked even more so as she came down the stairs with a struggling Flo in her arms. 'I'm afraid there's been a bit of an accident. Of course I'll replace the –'

'Please, don't bother,' snapped Mrs Brent. 'I'm most grateful to you for responding to Lucy's distress call and now I must get her some lunch.'

'I'll be off then,' said Mrs Jakes, looking downcast.

'Thanks for all your help.' Lucy was anxious that her helpful neighbour shouldn't feel shown up.

'That's all right, love. I'll take Flo home. And by the way, Mrs Brent –'

'Yes?' Her voice was grim.

'I'm afraid Flo got a little upset in a strange house and wet the upstairs carpet. Shall I do some cleaning up?'

'No need.' Mrs Brent closed her eyes against it all. 'Just let me attend to everything.' She turned to Lucy. 'Are you sure you're all right after that fall? No broken bones?'

'No,' replied Lucy. 'I was lucky.' She glanced across at Flo whose green eyes seemed to flicker back menacingly.

9

You see, I'm not safe anywhere...and now I'm having stupid thoughts about Flo but I'm just being ridiculous - I love that cat. I've checked myself again for injuries but I can't find anything at all except a few bruises. So I'm not going to die. Not yet anyway. But that Dark Man is really scaring me - sometimes it seems that I'm the only one who sees him. I can't help thinking that he's here to warn me of my impending death...

Lucy sat on the side of her bed, trying to work out what she was going to do next. She couldn't just sit around waiting for – for what? She had to do something.

Suddenly Lucy made up her mind. She had to go and talk to Jane. She knew she would have to admit to telling, but she *had* to know whether Jane had sent her the card or not. And this seemed the only way to find out. Besides, she wanted to apologise, to try and make peace with her. If only her conscience was clear, then maybe she could cope with the problem of the Dark Man.

Once she had made the decision, Lucy felt much better. All she had to do now was to persuade her mother that she wasn't ill any more and that she needed to see Jane. Lucy realised that this might be difficult.

'You can't go out,' said Mrs Brent firmly as she gave Lucy a light lunch of invalid food – steamed fish and then rice pudding. Yuk, she thought. The fish smelt horrible and tasted the same.

'I've *got* to get out. I'm going stir crazy at home, Mum.'

'Don't be so stupid. I told the school you were sick. And it's your birthday tomorrow. You don't want to spoil that outing.'

Lucy tried to be more inventive. 'I've got to see Jane,' she blurted out. Well, at least that was the truth, wasn't it?

'Jane Crow?'

'Everybody's being so horrible. No one will speak to her.'

'She did a rotten thing.'

'She's got to have *some* support. She's only got Sue and Dawn – and they're awful!'

Mrs Brent smiled. 'You're a very sweet person,

Lucy. Of course you must help Jane. But you can do that when you get back to school.'

Lucy looked out of the window. She was going to have to produce a much stronger reason for seeing Jane. 'Look – I didn't tell you before, but I'm really worried. She – she phoned when you were out and said she couldn't take the pressure any longer.'

'She phoned you from school?' Mrs Brent sounded surprised.

'I need to see her, Mum.'

'I thought you two weren't close any more.'

'But we are,' said Lucy with real feeling, suddenly aware that that was what she was hoping for in some strange, fantastical way. But surely, when Jane found out Lucy had told on her, she'd never speak to her again.

'I'll tell you what I'll do. I'll drive you over to Jane's later and then pick you up again.'

Lucy threw her arms around her mother. 'Thank you,' she said. She looked at her watch. Jane probably wouldn't be home from school for another couple of hours. But she could try ringing her mother at the shop to see what her plans were for tonight.

Lucy went to the phone in confused hope, until the small, sane but deeply irritating voice of reason swept into her head. How *could* she expect Jane to be friends with her again when she heard what she had done? And, anyway – she might well know already, hence the card and the sudden appearance of the Dark Man...

Lucy picked up the receiver, trying to stop herself thinking. Her brain was like a Catherine Wheel nailed to a fence post. Once the fuse was lit the wheel would spin until all you could see was a circle of fire. That was exactly how her mind felt.

'Who's calling?' Mrs Crow sounded tense and depressed.

'Lucy Brent.'

'Who?'

'Lucy Brent,' she faltered.

'Oh yes.' Mrs Crow's voice was dull and Lucy immediately wondered what she knew.

'Do you know what Jane's doing tonight. I'd like to see her if possible.'

'What for?'

'A chat.'

There was a brief silence. 'This is Jane's ice-skating evening and she'll be down at the rink.' She paused. 'You want to chat? I thought no one was speaking to Jane except Dawn and Sue. And to tell you the truth, I've never been that keen on those two.'

'I'm speaking to her,' said Lucy in delight. 'Maybe I'll drop by the rink.'

'I wish you would,' said Mrs Crow, suddenly showing the real desperation she must be feeling. 'I know she was in the wrong, but the more supporters she can get the better. Jane's never cheated before and never will again.'

'I know that, Mrs Crow.'

'I'd love to know who gave her away. Probably one of her closest friends.' She sounded bitter. 'One of her fair-weather friends.'

Lucy felt a sudden lurch of guilty despair. But somehow she ploughed on. '*I'd* like to support her.'

'Would you?' Mrs Crow sounded almost warm now. 'You used to be such friends. Jane will be down at the rink from about four. She's a wonderful skater,' she added proudly.

'I'll be there,' Lucy promised.

Her mother, however, was much harder to persuade. 'Someone's house, maybe,' she said. 'Where it's warm. But not down at that freezing cold ice rink. You'll catch your death.'

Lucy shuddered at the familiar phrase, so

unimportant to everyone else.

'I'll wrap up warm,' she pleaded. 'Jane's mother's so upset. I've got to give Jane my support.'

'All right.' Mrs Brent surprisingly gave in. 'But only on condition you wrap up very warm and I drive you there –'

'Thanks so –'

'I haven't finished yet. You can have a chat with Jane for twenty minutes while I wait outside.'

'Can't I stay longer?'

'No. I like what you're trying to do – but I can't run the risk of you getting really ill.'

'I *was* really ill,' said Lucy indignantly.

'Personally I think you're exhausted, but I won't argue. When do you want to go?'

'In an hour?'

'Your chauffeur will be waiting.'

Lucy felt a thrill of hope. Would Jane own up like she was going to? Could they both drive away the Dark Man?

10

I'm lying on my bed, counting the minutes until I can see Jane. I'm trying to keep calm but it's the waiting that's so difficult. I need to know if she wrote that card. I'm praying she did. But will Jane tell me, after I tell her what I did? I've just <u>got</u> to know. Wish me luck...I think I'm going to need it.

Mrs Crow was right. Jane was a brilliant skater and Lucy stood watching while she cut a figure of eight and then spun round on the spot. Soon she was skating at speed, swooping past the barrier where Lucy was standing. She could see Dawn and Sue on the ice, but they weren't nearly so good and kept returning to the barrier and clinging on.

All too aware of the limited time she had, and her mother waiting impatiently in the car outside, she self-consciously called Jane's name again and again.

Finally, Jane heard her calling and skated towards her with an impatient frown. 'What do *you* want?' she asked ungraciously.

'Just a – a quick word.'

'Well?'

Lucy found she couldn't raise the subject of the card immediately, and she stuttered out, 'I just wondered how you were.'

'What do you mean?'

'You must be lonely.' Too late, Lucy realised how patronising she must sound.

'I've got my friends – my true friends.'

'I think the others are wrong.' Lucy knew she was mishandling the situation and began to panic. Jane looked agitated and annoyed.

'What about?'

'Not talking to you.'

Jane finally lost her temper. 'Have you really come all this way to patronise me?'

'No!'

'Then what *are* you here for?'

'I thought you might like some company.'

'Not yours. So if you've quite finished –'

'I haven't just come to –' Lucy noticed that Jane was staring at her hard, still leaning on the barrier, without the slightest indication that she was going to skate off. She looked as if she was waiting for something to happen.

'What do you really want then?'

'Was it a joke?'

'Joke?'

'The card you sent me.'

There was a long pause while Lucy studied Jane's expression carefully, but she gave nothing away. Her eyes didn't even flicker.

'Why should I send you a card?' she asked casually.

'It was a joke, wasn't it? That Death Day card.'

Jane looked at Lucy in apparent amazement. 'Are you mad?' she asked. 'What do you *mean* – a Death Day card? Is there such a thing? I've never heard of it before.'

'Neither have I.'

'What did it say?'

'Happy Death Day.'

Jane stared at her in silence. Then she grinned, as if she had just heard a good joke but was reluctant to laugh out loud, and Lucy felt a stab of fear.

'*Did* you send it to me?'

'What if I did?' Jane was playing with her now and her grin widened. 'I'm not telling you anything – unless you tell me something too.'

Lucy paused. This was the moment for her confession. Why was she putting it off?

'Why should I?' Jane half whispered. 'Why

should I send *you* a card – of all people?'

Despite the chill of the rink, Lucy began to sweat.

'I still don't know who gave me away.' Jane spoke so softly that Lucy could hardly hear her. 'It couldn't be you, could it?'

There was a long, long silence.

'You were just jealous, weren't you?' demanded Jane. 'Hoping you'd put me in my place.'

Lucy wanted to run away and keep on running. But she also knew that if she lost this opportunity she wouldn't get another one. She had set it all up. She couldn't back off now.

'I wasn't hoping to catch you out, but I saw the answers to the exam on your arm in the loo. So I told Mrs Greenway.' Lucy felt a flood of relief. At last she had spoken out, at last she had made the confession and she could feel clean again. But Lucy had not reckoned on Jane's reaction.

The smile on Jane's face was fixed and rigid, and her eyes were full of venom as she drew back her right hand and hit Lucy a stinging slap around the face. Then she hit her again.

Lucy staggered backwards and some of the skaters, including Dawn and Sue, turned to glance curiously at the two girls.

'I'm sorry.' Lucy turned her face away. The tears stinging her eyes were almost as painful as the weals on her cheek.

'I shouldn't have cheated, should I? You only did your duty.' Jane was sneering now.

'Did you send me the card?'

'What if I did?' Jane asked again and this time her smile was triumphant.

'*Please* tell me.' Lucy was desperate. Surely her confession meant something? 'We had a bargain, didn't we? I've told you what I did. Now you've got to tell me.'

'Bargain? Why should we have a bargain?' Jane paused. 'There's only one way you're going to find out about that card.'

'How?'

'Come on the ice.'

'But you know I can't skate.'

'I'll teach you.' Jane's expression was blank, impossible to interpret.

'No –'

'Why not?'

'I don't want to go on the ice. I'm afraid of falling.' Suddenly, the terror was back. Was this the next trap? Lucy gazed wildly about her, searching desperately for an escape route.

'I'll hang on to you.'

'I've already fallen down the stairs this morning. I'm covered in bumps and bruises.'

'That was clumsy of you.'

'I tripped over a black cat.'

'Bad luck on the black cat.'

'*Did* you send me that card?'

'What if I did?'

'You've *got* to tell me.'

'I haven't got to tell you anything,' said Jane, though she seemed friendlier now. 'But I will if you come on the ice. I've got a spare pair of skates over there.'

'They won't fit me.'

'Yes they will. I think they'll fit you perfectly.'

'You'll look after me?' Lucy was terrified, but she knew she couldn't back out now. She simply had to find out whether Jane had sent the card, whatever the risk might be.

'All the time. Come and join the gang.'

But Lucy didn't want to do that. She didn't want to be sent up by Dawn and Sue. Then she made her painful decision. 'OK. I'll come, but I don't want to be with them. I want to be with you. Just like we used to be.'

Jane grinned. 'It'll just be us,' she promised.

*

Jane held her hand, just like a good friend would, and slowly, very slowly, led Lucy on to the ice, avoiding the other skaters, avoiding Dawn and Sue, grabbing her in a strong, safe grip whenever she showed the least sign of falling over. They were together again, Lucy thought. Why not just abandon herself to Jane's responsibility? She was determined to believe in her. Here they were together again. Here they were friends again. She must treasure the moment.

Slowly Lucy felt more confident, giving herself over to Jane's care, letting herself trust her. She felt strangely secure and happy, but at the same time she was trying to be logical, wondering if Jane really was going to be her friend again. Could such a thing be possible, despite all Lucy had done to her?

Jane put her arm around her waist and slowly and patiently began to teach her to skate. Gradually Lucy gathered a little confidence and soon they were both progressing slowly and carefully around the edge of the rink.

'Am I doing OK?' Lucy bellowed over the canned music and the shouts of the other skaters.

'You're doing perfectly,' said Jane. 'So perfectly

that we're going to be a bit more ambitious – aren't we, Lucy?'

'Are we?' Apprehension abruptly returned. Then, just as they were coming round the rink for the fifth time, Lucy saw him.

She couldn't make out whether the Dark Man was carrying something over his shoulder or not as he limped up the steps of the rink towards the exit. She wasn't even sure whether it was definitely him. It could have been anyone. He didn't look back and was soon out of sight.

'Why, Lucy,' said Jane almost tenderly. 'What's the matter? You're trembling. Don't you trust me any more?'

'I thought I saw someone I knew.'

'Someone you're frightened of?'

'Well – yes.'

'Why's that?'

'I don't really know.' Lucy felt a complete fool. How could she possibly tell Jane about the Dark Man? She was bound to laugh and then their renewed friendship would be over.

Without warning, Jane increased her speed, and within seconds Lucy was being whirled round the ice so fast she could hardly see straight. She began to feel giddy and the rink around her became a blur.

'Stop!' she yelled.

But Jane only skated faster, holding Lucy in a strong grip from which she was quite unable to pull herself free.

'You've got to stop!'

Lucy felt sick now and knew that she was completely out of control. What was Jane going to do? Suppose she let her go? She felt as if she was on a roundabout that was going far too fast, and the blur intensified until all she could see were dark swirling shapes.

Then, just as suddenly as she had started, Jane began to slow down until they were stationary at the edge of the rink. Dawn and Sue were there. They were both laughing.

Lucy reached out and clung to the barrier, gasping for breath, the ice slowly coming back into focus, the sick and giddy feeling slowly dropping away.

'What did you do that for?' Lucy stuttered. 'You said you'd keep me safe.'

'I did keep you safe.' Jane's eyes were mocking.

'She kept you *very* safe,' Sue spluttered.

'You were going at the speed of light,' sneered Dawn. 'Lucky Jane protected you.'

'And you said you'd tell me if you sent that card,' yelled Lucy, unable to control her anger and fear.

'What if I did?' Jane asked yet again. 'What if I did?'

Lucy stumbled away from the ice and tore off the skates. The fantasy was over – it was obvious that Jane didn't care about her now, and never, ever would. What a fool she'd been to confess and then to have all her hopes destroyed. She deserved all she'd got. Even worse, she had discovered nothing. Would she ever know if Jane had sent her the card? Lucy dragged on her shoes, desperate to get away, but she was in such a blind panic that she couldn't find the exit, running in circles, just as her mind had done.

Meanwhile, Jane slowly and effortlessly skated alongside her. 'What if I did?' she kept repeating. 'What if I did?'

Lucy was beginning to bump into people now and her giddiness returned. Her mind was full of terrifying thoughts. Jane had sent the Dark Man and the Dark Man had sent Flo to send her crashing down the stairs. So far she had survived, but of course the Dark Man and Flo had been playing with her, just like Jane. Soon, however, Lucy was sure the game would stop and they would come for her in earnest.

As Lucy ran on, desperately searching for the exit, she ran straight into someone coming the other way. She looked up to see a huge bearded giant of a man, with a pair of skates under his arm and a whining child pulling at his jacket.

'Steady on, young lady. Where are you running to in such a hurry?'

'I'm looking for the way out,' she gasped.

'It's up the staircase.'

'Thanks.'

'Think nothing of it.'

He smiled while the child continued to whimper, 'I want to go back on the ice again. I want to go back on the ice.'

Lucy came to a breathless halt at the top of the stairs and turned to watch Jane lazily circling the ice, a hand raised in languid farewell. Then Jane rejoined Sue and Dawn and Lucy could hear her laughter, much louder than the others, resounding around the rink.

Lucy hurried out of the doors into the deadly cold of the night. A terrifying world awaited her. Boys on skateboards came too near, the traffic roared threateningly, a girl in a tracksuit almost collided with her, shop fronts glittered menacingly, hard merciless light beamed down from lampposts, a cyclist zoomed past and a motorbike shrieked to a halt as she crossed the road. Lucy realised that like the car the other day she hadn't even seen the biker bearing down on her. She didn't stand a chance.

Somehow she reached her mother's car in the lay-by and thankfully got in beside her.

'What's the matter? You look so ill. I should never have agreed to this.' Mrs Brent was partly condemning, partly concerned.

'I'm OK.' Lucy tried to sound casual, despite her heaving chest.

'Did you see Jane?'

Lucy nodded. 'We had a talk.'

'You don't look as if it went that well.'

'It didn't.'

'I'm sorry.'

'And I want to tell you why it didn't. You see –' Lucy knew she should never have confessed to Jane. She was the wrong person. She should have told her mother directly it had happened. But Lucy still hesitated. Was she ashamed? There was a long, tense silence. Then she suddenly burst into a torrent of words. 'You see – I was the one who told on her.'

'The exam?' Her mother was astounded.

'I saw her cheating.'

'But she didn't realise –'

'No.'

'Why *did* you tell her?' Mrs Brent seemed deeply worried now.

'I just had to be honest.'

'And what was her reaction?'

'She was OK at first. Then she said she'd teach me to skate.'

'In the circumstances,' Mrs Brent said drily, 'that was pretty big of her, wasn't it?'

'But she went out of her way to be scary.'

'That's hardly surprising.' Her mother sat behind the wheel, staring ahead, without starting up the engine.

'Mum, did I do the right thing by reporting Jane to Mrs Greenway? I mean – what would you have done?'

'I'm not sure,' replied her mother thoughtfully. 'I think I would have spoken to Jane herself, told her to own up to Mrs Greenway.'

'Would you?'

'Probably.'

'But suppose she refused?'

'Then I'd have got other students to put pressure on her.'

'So I *was* wrong.'

'I'm not saying that. You made a decision.' Mrs Brent paused. 'Is that why you've been so down in the dumps? Is that why you've been ill?'

'Yes,' Lucy said miserably.

'Why didn't you tell me earlier?'

'I couldn't.'

'Is there anything else you want to say?'

Lucy thought hurriedly. The card? The Dark Man? But if she told her, she was certain her mother would only claim she was suffering from guilt and that everything was in her imagination.

'No,' she said at last. Mrs Brent glanced at her daughter anxiously. 'Let's go home.' She started up the car. 'Now look, Lucy. You're not going to get yourself into a state over this, are you?'

'I just feel so bad about it all.'

'It's done now – and I'm sure everything will blow over in a week or so. You're just going to have to sit it out.'

'Am I?' Lucy was slightly sulky now.

'Why don't you look on the bright side?'

'What bright side?'

'You've got the school trip tomorrow. Surely you haven't forgotten? After all – it *is* your birthday.'

Lucy certainly hadn't forgotten that tomorrow was her birthday. Her Death Day.

'I can't go!' She shivered, the panic sweeping through her. A coach journey. Anything could happen. But she also realised it wouldn't be safe to stay at home either – not after what she had experienced today.

'I've paid good money for that trip,' snapped Mrs Brent. 'Besides, it'll do you good. You know how much you were looking forward to going.'

But that was weeks ago, thought Lucy. When the world was a different place.

'I don't want to go.'

'Why ever not?'

'Because Jane will be there.'

'And so will dozens of other boys and girls. Come on, Lucy – you don't have to sit next to her.'

'They'll all know what I've done now.'

'Why?'

'Because Jane will spread it round the whole school.' There was a long silence between them before Lucy spoke again. 'I can't face them. You told me yourself you'd have handled it differently.'

'I don't know *what* I would have done. But either way, you can't go on like this.'

'Like what?'

'Hiding.'

Lucy grimly realised that her mother was right. If she stayed at home she would only be watching at the window, waiting for the Dark Man's next appearance. Maybe she *would* be safer on the coach, despite what they all might say.

'So what are you going to do?' asked Mrs Brent impatiently.

Lucy sighed. She knew she was beaten. Mum had paid out a lot of money for the price of the coach and the theatre ticket. 'All right. I'll go, but don't blame me if they're *all* nasty to me.'

'Why should they be?' Mrs Brent tried to be reasonable. 'What Jane did was wrong and I'm sure she knows that. What she really needs is to get on with her life, and so do you. Then everyone stands a chance of putting this wretched business behind them.'

*

I feel much better now that I've told someone, even though it was my mother. And I'm glad I've told Jane too, despite the fact that she didn't own up to sending me the card. I've just got to get a grip on the situation and control my fears. There's a rational explanation for everything...well, almost everything.

Lucy stood by her bedroom window and watched and waited. Talking to her mother in the car and making the decision about going to the theatre had made her more confident, although she couldn't think why. Perhaps her new-found confidence had come about because of her confession to Jane and the relief of admitting it all?

Whatever the cause, Lucy felt determined, promising herself that if the Dark Man approached the house she would confront him, demand to know what he was up to, ringing her doorbell and casually waving like that. Did he live in the snow-bound woods? To Lucy's knowledge there were no houses on the hill, not even a hut, but perhaps he slept rough. Or did he use the woodland path as a short cut? But the more Lucy considered a logical explanation the more far-fetched it seemed, and soon her spirits plunged to a new low. The Dark Man was supernatural, the messenger of death, who was about to claim her life. And that was it.

Lucy waited for a long time, watching the darkness, but there was no sign of him. The snow had stopped falling, replaced by a hard frost, making the frozen landscape glint and glitter in a harsh, menacing way.

Then she heard the sound of an engine and at the same time the telephone began to ring. Ignoring the phone, she watched as a fish and chip van drew up outside the house with an illuminated sign proclaiming *Frying Tonight*.

Dimly she heard her mother shouting into the telephone, 'What? You mean you're *not* coming home tonight? Where are you going? It's her birthday tomorrow –' To try and block out the sound, Lucy opened the window and the most succulent smell of fish and chips wafted into her room, making her realise how ravenously hungry she was.

Wondering if her mother had suddenly ordered up a treat, she ran downstairs only to hear the row between her parents reaching a crescendo of anger and bitterness.

'Don't bother to come back then,' shouted her

mother. 'We're both happy on our own.'

Lucy winced, but she was still consumed by hunger and darted to the door as the bell rang, imagining the thick, crispy batter and the soft, flaky fish. The smell was delicious. She would add some salt and masses of tomato ketchup. She pulled open the front door eagerly, unprepared for what she saw.

11

'The name's Ted Turner. Your friendly neighbourhood fish and chippy.'

But Lucy was gazing past him, staring at the figure lurking by the van. She could see the Dark Man's bony face, flesh stretched tight, so tight that she could almost see his skin peeling away down to the skull beneath. With a chill of horror she realised there was an object slung over his shoulder, covered in what looked like oilcloth. Was he really carrying a scythe? The Dark Man turned and smiled at her, stretching his skin even tighter.

In the hall, Lucy could still hear her mother arguing with her father on the phone.

'I haven't seen you round here before,' Lucy said to Ted Turner, looking over his shoulder, her gaze locked into the Dark Man's deep eye sockets. Did he *have* eyes? *Happy Death Day*. Tomorrow was her thirteenth birthday. *Happy Death Day*.

'I'm trying to increase my territory. It's all fresh fish frying out there, you know.' Ted Turner paused and looked back at his van. 'Oi!' he yelled. 'You get out of there. Like now! Just push off.'

The Dark Man turned and limped away, back down the road towards the hill.

'Who is he?' gasped Lucy.

'Just an old tramp, – a vagrant who's suddenly shown up in the area. He seems to like the smell of fish and chips. I've had cause to have a go at him before, despite the fact I *do* sometimes give him the odd bag of chips. Fancy him coming all the way up here.'

Lucy didn't know whether to be relieved or even more afraid. Was the Dark Man really a harmless vagrant? What about that thing on his back?

'What's he wearing?' she asked abruptly.

'That old overcoat. I know it's –'

'I mean – what's he wearing on his back?'

'Oh, I see what you mean. I asked him that.'

'Did he tell you?' Lucy demanded impatiently.

'Said he'd had an accident and that he had to wear this brace over his shoulders and down his back. I feel sorry for him, but he puts the customers off. Can I tempt you to –'

'Do you know his name?'

Ted Turner looked at Lucy impatiently, anxious to make a sale. 'Haven't a clue, love. I came up your way before and rang the bell but no one was in.'

'I've seen that tramp walking down the hill,' said Lucy insistently.

Ted Turner gave her an appraising look. 'There's nothing to worry about. I'm sure he's harmless.'

Just then, Mrs Jakes hurried up the path. Lucy kept a close look out for Flo, but the black cat didn't seem to be with her.

'Hello, dear. How are you? Feeling a little better now?'

'I'm fine,' said Lucy.

'I'm so sorry about that business with Flo. Not too many bruises, I hope?'

'I'm OK,' Lucy replied, all too conscious of Ted Turner's mounting curiosity.

'So you're making a stop here now, are you?' asked Mrs Jakes enthusiastically.

'If there's enough trade.' Ted was cautious.

'I've got four starving kids at home,' she explained. 'And a husband with a bottomless pit for a stomach.'

'That'll make a start.' Ted smiled triumphantly.

Mrs Brent came to the door, looking hot and flushed and unhappy. 'Now what's going on?'

'Name's Ted Turner. Just checking out new territory.'

'I beg your pardon?' Mrs Brent was annoyed to see Mrs Jakes standing at her front door as well.

'Fish and chips,' explained Mrs Jakes, not in the least put out. 'Can't you smell 'em?'

'Not today, thank you.'

'They're fresh,' pleaded Ted. 'And your daughter looks hungry.'

'She's had her tea,' said Mrs Brent firmly, starting to close the door.

'Hold on. I've got a message for someone called Lucy. Is that you?'

Lucy immediately felt sick with fright. Was Ted Turner another of the Dark Man's messengers? Like Flo?

'Really?' asked Mrs Brent.

'It's all meant to be a bit of a surprise.' Ted gazed at Lucy thoughtfully. 'I saw your friend earlier – she's a regular customer – and when I told her I was going to make a pitch in Laurel Avenue she asked me to be a postman.'

'Wouldn't it have been easier to phone?' demanded Lucy in bewilderment, wondering who on earth he was talking about but somehow not wanting to ask.

'I'm well-known round these parts,' said Ted proudly. 'I carry lots of messages between my customers. So when someone asks me to drop one round, I'm only too happy to oblige.'

He was staring at her as if he needed payment and Lucy, with no appetite at all now, felt she should make the message worth carrying.

'Can I have some chips?' she asked dolefully.

Her mother sighed. 'You'll have fish as well. Eating chips is unhealthy.'

'And yourself, madam?' asked Ted. 'Can I tempt you?'

'No, thank you.' Mrs Brent compressed her lips.

'*I'll* have six double cod and chips,' broke in Mrs Jakes.

'This is my lucky night,' said Ted Turner as he returned to his van. 'That's the kind of order that makes the journey worthwhile.'

As Mrs Jakes started to ask about Lucy's health the telephone began to ring again, and Mrs Brent took great pleasure in slamming the front door in her face.

'If that's your father again –' Mrs Brent hurried threateningly to the phone while Lucy watched her, her thoughts in turmoil. An icy chill spread through her and then increased as her mother, holding a hand to the receiver, whispered,

'It's Jane Crow for you.'

Lucy approached the telephone fearfully. Could Jane and the Grim Reaper be working together? Did he have a gang like Jane did? A gang that included a black cat and a man who sold fish and chips?

'Hello, Jane?' Lucy's voice shook.

'You coming to the theatre tomorrow?'

'Yes.'

'Couldn't lend me some money, could you?' She sounded friendly but awkward.

'Money? What for?' Lucy was startled. What kind of trick was she playing now?

'I got my allowance taken away for a fortnight as a punishment. I expect you know why. So I'm a couple of pounds short for the trip and I need a friend. Dawn and Sue soon melt away if it's a question of money.'

'I don't think I count as a friend any more,' said Lucy bitterly. 'Especially after what I did to you. Still, you took your revenge, didn't you?'

'I was only teasing down at the ice rink. I'm sorry.'

Strangely, Jane sounded genuinely penitent and, as a result, Lucy heard herself saying, 'I'll lend you the money.'

'Thanks. I really appreciate that.' She sounded less friendly now that her request had been granted.

'By the way,' said Lucy. 'Did you send me a message?'

'No.'

'Via the fish and chip man?'

'Of course not.'

'His name's Ted Turner.'

'And I'm Minnie Mouse.' Jane giggled. 'I don't usually send messages via fish and chip men. See you tomorrow.'

The front door bell rang again.

'Can you get it?' yelled Mum. 'I'm going to have a bath. There's some money on the kitchen table. But don't encourage that man to come back.'

'Why not?'

'It's bad enough with Mrs Jakes next door. We don't want a fish and chip van in the avenue too, do we?'

Depressed by her mother's snobbery, and still trying to work out the mystery of the message, Lucy opened the door to find Ted Turner clutching the newspaper-wrapped fish and chips – and an envelope. He handed both over with a cheerful grin and accepted the money Lucy held out to him.

'Mrs Jakes tells me it's your birthday tomorrow.'

'Yes,' said Lucy warily.

'Happy –' he hesitated fractionally, 'birthday for tomorrow then.'

'Thanks.'

'Enjoy your fish and chips.' Ted Turner waved casually and strolled back to his van.

Lucy stood on the doorstep, kicking herself for letting him go. Why hadn't she confronted him, insisted on knowing who had sent the message. But it was too late now and the opportunity had been missed.

Lucy dumped her fish and chips on the kitchen table and ripped open the envelope. The card felt like a slither of ice in her grip and she immediately dropped it on the floor. Lucy gazed down, wanting to leave the thing where it was.

Eventually, she forced herself to pick up the card and slowly and hesitantly turned it over. Then she went to the kitchen sink and was violently sick.

The card read: HAPPY DEATH DAY, LUCY

An engraving of the Grim Reaper had again been stuck to the bottom of the card and Lucy couldn't help noticing how like the old tramp he looked.

She ran back to the front door, wrenched it open and gazed down the dark, icy avenue. It was deserted.

my new-found confidence has vanished. I've just received another Death Day card. Why is someone doing this to me? I don't want to go to sleep as I know I'll dream of the ivy-covered grave in the woods. But the more I try to keep awake, the more I keep dozing off. And tomorrow it's my birthday and it's going to be terrible. Everyone will know I told on Jane and they'll all hate and despise me. I'll be even more unpopular than she is. But what does that matter? I'm going to die anyway. Will this be my last diary entry?

That night Lucy dreamt about the Dark Man. He was walking down the hill, wearing a hooded cloak, with his scythe openly held under one arm. He looked up at her, pushing his hood aside and exposing a skull where his gaunt features had once been. His eye sockets blazed as he walked to her front door and rang the bell, which blasted her ears with a thin metallic sound like a dentist's drill.

Lucy woke with a start, her mouth dry, her heart

pounding. She sat up in bed, gripping the sheets, remembering every detail of the dream, grateful at least that she had not been taken along the path to the ivy-covered grave.

'Lucy!' her mother bellowed from downstairs. 'We've overslept. Happy birthday. You'll have to open your presents tonight or you'll be late for school.'

Lucy struggled out of bed and gazed down at her bedroom carpet. The Death Day cards lay face up, with their threatening words and pictures staring up at her. How had they got there?

'Lucy!' yelled her mother. 'You've got ten minutes to leave the house!'

'Happy birthday, darling. You're a teenager! Isn't that marvellous?' Mrs Brent kissed her daughter as she helped Lucy on with her coat. 'As it's an afternoon performance, you shouldn't be back too late, and then we'll have a lovely birthday tea and you can unwrap your presents.'

'What about Dad?' Lucy asked anxiously, despite the fact that she had hardly given him a thought.

'What about him?' Mrs Brent looked nervous.

'Is he coming home tonight?'

Her mother sighed. 'I suppose you heard that

row we had last night.'

'Bits of it.'

'Well – we've got no time to talk now. But, yes, he'll be coming home for your birthday.'

'You promise?'

Mrs Brent hesitated. Then she nodded, 'I promise.'

Directly she closed the front door, the terror seized Lucy even more strongly. *Happy Death Day.* The words beat in her mind over and over again as she walked down the garden path, wiping out any hope of surviving she might have had left.

The traffic seemed heavier and faster than ever. Trucks roared past, so near to the pavement that Lucy found herself hugging the shop fronts, almost touching the glass. Aircraft droned low overhead, and on one corner roadworks had been set up and a man in goggles was breaking up the tarmac with a juddering drill.

As Lucy hurried past he seemed to turn towards her and the drill gnawed at the pavement only a metre or so from her feet. The noisy vibration was awful and Lucy was sure the drill was edging closer to her by the second. This is it, she thought. This is my Death Day. Soon the drill would be biting into her feet, pinning her to the pavement as she bled to death.

Sparks flew and Lucy ran, not looking where she was going. Without thinking, desperate to get away, she plunged into the road and a van shrieked to a halt with a squeal of tyres, just missing her. Lucy stood trembling, fighting back her tears, unable to move, the drill still vibrating in her ears.

The driver wound down his window and yelled, 'You're an idiot, aren't you? What are you? An idiot!' He was young and looked almost as frightened as she did. As he drove off Lucy glanced at the side of the van and saw the sign: *William De'Ath – Undertaker*.

She walked unsteadily on towards school. De'Ath was only an apostrophe away from Death. There could be no doubt about what was happening. The Dark Man was still playing with her just like Jane had. How long would the game last? Surely time was running out.

By the time Lucy arrived at school, her thoughts were running in the by now familiar vicious circle. The day was less cold and some of the snow in the playground was melting into dirty grey puddles. She sat through her classes gloomily, yet was still surprised when Jane never so much as gave her a glance, going out of her way to avoid Lucy at break, without asking for the loan. But she was also surprised that Jane apparently hadn't told anyone that she had grassed on her. Lucy had already met some of her classmates and they seemed far too casual – even friendly – to know.

Eventually she came across Jane in the corridor, thankfully without her handmaidens Sue and Dawn. Lucy grabbed her by the arm. 'Don't you want the loan?' she asked reproachfully.

'No, thanks.'

'But you phoned and –'

'It's OK now. My mother gave me what I needed.'

'But I thought she'd taken away your allowance until –'

'This is really none of your business.' Jane was dismissive.

'You *made* it my business.'

They stared at each other, Lucy with bewilderment and Jane with her usual mocking contempt.

'So you're punishing me again.'

'Think what you like.' Jane began to hurry on. 'Just stop bothering me, that's all.'

Lucy turned away, her eyes full of tears.

After lunch the theatre party boarded the coach with Mrs Greenway and Mrs Beacon in charge.

'Now, I want you all to enjoy yourselves,' said Mrs Greenway over the tannoy. 'But make sure you're wearing your safety belts, and I don't want any stupid behaviour. The roads are in bad condition and the driver has got to concentrate.' She sat down and the coach moved slowly away.

Lucy, who was sitting next to a girl called Jill, glanced round to see where Jane was, finally spotting her at the front, next to Dawn. Sue was just opposite, beside Mrs Beacon who was talking to Mrs Greenway. Jane was staring blankly out of the window, seemingly dejected. But Lucy felt no triumph. Instead she still wanted to reach out to Jane, to offer her friendship.

The coach ground on, traffic overtaking, the driver steering cautiously in a low gear, and Lucy felt her heart sink as she realised the route he was taking. Eventually they would pass her own house and, worse still, the wooded hill. She began to feel the familiar coldness inside. The grave from her dream was somewhere out there in the undergrowth and Lucy gazed out of the window until the path the

Dark Man had trodden came into view.

The sun had come out, but the road was in the shade of the hill and the surface had had no chance to thaw. The driver changed down to an even lower gear as the coach slowly climbed.

Lucy gazed down at the dense woodland that was still shrouded in snow. The winter sun hadn't penetrated the trees which were bleak and menacing. And somewhere the ivy-covered grave waited for her, she was sure of that.

Then Lucy made a last and supreme effort to be rational. The grave was just part of a dream, created by her own anxiety. But she still looked down at the frozen woodland and shuddered.

The driver changed gear again as the coach breasted the hill and slowly began to crawl down the other side.

Suddenly there was a jolt and a clash of gears and Lucy had the feeling that the heavy vehicle had suddenly speeded up. Moments later, there was another jolt, but she still didn't react and neither did anyone else as the excited chatter increased.

It wasn't until Jill began to scream in the seat beside her that Lucy realised something was badly wrong and she felt the coach skid across the road.

Lucy turned to look at Jill whose mouth was wide open as she screamed and screamed again. Other pupils were crying out now as the panic spread and, staring down, she saw the tops of the snow-bound trees. The coach continued to skid, the driver fighting for control, and Lucy realised with dread that the brakes were locked.

Suddenly, they were nearing the left–hand side of the road again, and although there was a crash barrier, the drop below was sheer.

Happy Death Day. Lucy's mind was filled with the words. *Happy Death Day.* The Dark Man's games were over. This was it.

Her gaze returned to the interior of the sliding coach and she saw that Jane had turned and was staring at her fixedly. Everyone was screaming now – except for her and Jane. They were sharing a special understanding – a knowledge that retribution could have come for both of them.

As the coach slid towards the drop the screaming grew louder. Cars hooted on the other side of the road as it scraped along the side of the crash barrier with the dreadful sound of rending metal.

Suddenly the barrier gave way and the coach slid sideways, rolling over until it was the right way up again and falling towards the snow-covered trees. Inside the screams intensified, but the seat belts kept the pupils in their seats.

Then the coach hit the tree tops, plunging through the branches with a grinding of metal and breaking glass. Seats were wrenched out of place, the luggage rack was torn off, nearly hitting Lucy, schoolbags were hurled about and the smell of diesel filtered the interior like a dense cloud. We're all going to burn, thought Lucy, and if we don't we'll be crushed instead.

Then she saw someone literally flying through the air and watched with horrified amazement as Jane was flung through a broken window. Hadn't she been wearing her seat belt, Lucy wondered, numbed now by the unbelievable terror of what was happening.

The coach continued to fall, with more windows breaking and more bags falling from the racks. Then there was a final splintering, rending, tearing sound as they came to rest amidst fallen trees. Lucy's belt restrained her throughout, but the dislodged seat in front caught her head as they landed and a wall of blackness came hurtling towards her.

*

Lucy stirred and felt blood on her forehead. The coach was lying at an angle and its passengers were groaning or crying or sitting staring ahead, either unconscious or – Lucy didn't want to think about that. Strangely, impossibly, she was alive. But for how long?

She turned to the broken window beside her and saw she was covered in shattered fragments of glass. Wiping them away, she peered out at the tangled foliage which had cushioned their landing.

Unfastening her seat belt without thinking what she was going to do, Lucy staggered to her feet, trying to cope with the angle the coach was lying at, still surprised that she was alive. Wasn't this her Death Day? But nothing seemed to be hurting except her head. She wiped away some of the blood and looked around unseeingly in the semi-darkness. The smell of diesel was much stronger now.

Lucy craned her neck through the broken window and suddenly saw Jane lying on her back outside. Was she alive? Lucy knew she had to get out. She had to help Jane. But how?

Lucy could hear creaking sounds from outside as the broken branches took the weight of the coach. The window opposite her was smashed, like most of the others, and the seats were empty. Could she reach Jane? What kind of a drop would there be? Or could she climb down the tangled trees? Lucy was sure the coach was unstable and if the vehicle rolled over Jane would be crushed to death. She *had* to reach her somehow.

Jane was lying a little to the right of an ivy-covered mound and Lucy paused apprehensively. Wasn't that mound familiar? But she had no time to try and remember. So far she had escaped serious injury, but what might happen to her if she started climbing out of the unstable coach on to equally unstable broken branches? Anything could give way and they might *both* be crushed.

As Lucy wrestled with her dilemma, Jill stirred in the seat beside her.

'What happened?' she muttered.

'There's been an accident,' Lucy replied bleakly.

'Are we going to be OK?' Jill asked, childishly dependent.

'We seem to be. I don't know about the others, though.' Lucy decided against telling Jill about the instability of the wrecked vehicle and the shaky support beneath.

'OK, everybody. I'm not sure who's hurt and who's not –' Mrs Greenway's voice was shaky but commanding.

There was a reassuring muttering as some pupils claimed to be unhurt. But not everybody replied.

'Thank God for the seat belts,' continued Mrs Greenway. 'But now I want you to try and sit as quietly as possible. As far as I can see, we're only being supported by fallen trees and branches and the coach could still roll over.' Her voice faltered for a moment and then she regained control. 'The accident must have been seen from the road and help should be on its way.' She paused. 'Mrs Beacon's unconscious and so is the driver, and as we could be here for some time, you *must* sit still.'

A few pupils began to sob quietly and then a siren began to wail in the distance.

'Miss,' shouted Lucy, standing up.

'Who's that?'

'Lucy Brent.'

'Are you all right?'

'Yes, but Jane Crow isn't. She's been thrown out.'

'Can you see if she's moving at all?'

'Not from here, but I can easily climb out of a window.'

'You're *not* to move,' said Mrs Greenway insistently. 'You're to stay where you are.'

'If the coach rolls over, Jane's going to get crushed.'

'I told you to stay where you are.' Mrs Greenway sounded very angry now and Lucy sat down again. Then they all heard a snapping sound and the vehicle swayed slightly for a few seconds and resettled.

'I've got to get to Jane.' Lucy defiantly stood up again as the sirens got louder.

'Sit down!' shouted Mrs Greenway.

But Lucy was already scrambling over the seats opposite and up the slope caused by the angle of the coach to the window. Taking care to avoid the shattered glass, she somehow squeezed through unscathed, out on to the snow-covered branches of a fallen tree.

She was about three metres from the ground and although the coach began to creak and groan again, Lucy prayed there wasn't any immediate danger. She scrambled on, down the twisted branches, until she reached the ground where Jane was lying so still.

Lucy could hear Mrs Greenway calling her, but took no notice. Looking back, she could see the coach above her at its unstable angle. Suddenly, fear got the better of her, and she found herself unable to move, as if one footstep might crack one little twig that might crack another, setting up a chain reaction which would send the coach plunging down on top of Jane.

There was no birdsong, nor the slightest rustle in the undergrowth. Then the stillness was broken by the all too familiar creaking sound.

Lucy watched the coach begin to slowly and very gently sway again until miraculously it resettled. She stared up at one of the still intact windows. Was that a beaky shadow of a face pressed to the glass? Had the Dark Man been on board all the time?

Then Lucy dimly heard Mrs Greenway's shakily commanding voice, insisting once again that no one must move.

Forcing herself forward at last, Lucy stumbled across the uneven ground towards Jane, wondering whether there was anything she could do to help her, or if she was already dead? As she knelt down, Jane shifted slightly and Lucy saw that her face was covered in blood. Looking more closely, she could see that some of the glass from the coach window had become embedded in Jane's face. Would she be scarred for life, Lucy wondered in real horror. Jane had been so beautiful. Would she never be beautiful again? Then she noticed one of Jane's legs was at a strange angle, but Jane's eyes were wide open and a hand was faintly twitching. Lucy knew she mustn't touch Jane, let alone move her.

Lucy looked up fearfully at the coach again but its menacing bulk was still, at least for the moment.

'Jane?'

There was no reply and her eyes had closed again.

'Jane? Can you hear me? You've got to listen to me. Look at me!'

Jane's eyes slowly opened again and her lips moved but no words came.

'I know you're hurt, but you've *got* to lie still. The coach keeps swaying and –'

'What – coach –' she asked faintly.

Then the creaking sound above them seemed to intensify and Lucy knew that, whatever damage she might do, she *had* to move Jane.

'It might hurt some more, but if you stay here you're in terrible danger. I'm going to pull you away from the coach.'

Jane finally looked up and gasped, and Lucy felt a rush of apprehension. Suppose she killed her?

Suppose it was Jane's Death Day and not hers? Had the Dark Man got his victims mixed up?

Jane was trying to say something again and Lucy finally made out her words with some difficulty.

'I took off my seat belt.'

'When?'

'I knew we were going to crash.' Jane was a little clearer now.

'So why take off your seat belt?' Lucy was completely bewildered.

'I wanted to die.'

'You can't mean that.' Lucy knew she should be *doing* something, not talking. But once again she felt rooted to the spot, unable to take any action. 'I've come to help you. I climbed down out of the coach when –'

'I've got nothing to live for. Everyone knows I'm a cheat.' Jane was weaker now, her voice indistinct, and Lucy could only just hear.

'You've got me,' she said loudly. 'It was all my fault. I'm sorry I told on you. It was just some horrible impulse –'

Jane closed her eyes and Lucy felt a sense of total failure as well as rejection. But at least her limbs were working again.

'I'm going to pull you gently. Really gently.

Just a tiny bit at a time.'

Jane's eyes remained closed and Lucy wondered, with a sense of utter misery, if she *had* died. She took her wrist and felt for a pulse. To Lucy's intense relief it was beating quite strongly. With renewed hope and energy, she grabbed Jane's arms and began to pull her along.

'Am I hurting you?'

There was no response.

'I'll slow down.'

Lifting aside the broken wood, Lucy made the ground as smooth as she could and then returned to Jane, beginning to pull at her again. Several times she gave a soft gasp of pain.

Exhausted, Lucy took a short rest.

'Thank you,' whispered Jane.

'I thought you didn't want to live. That you wanted to give up.'

'I was lonely. I've sussed out Dawn and Sue. They're ghastly. They're so vindictive and gossipy, always trying to spite someone. I made a big mistake choosing them as friends. I'd rather have no friends than them – but I feel so alone now.'

'So do I,' snapped Lucy. 'How would you feel if you'd been sent two Happy Death Day cards? How would you like –'

As she spoke, she saw members of the fire brigade beginning to clamber down the steep-sided valley with ropes and tackle.

'Leave her where she is,' yelled one of the officers.

'I've got to drag her clear,' Lucy shouted back.

'We'll have the coach secure soon. If you go on pulling, you could do serious damage.'

As Lucy looked up defiantly, Jane whispered something she couldn't make out.

'I – want – to – tell – you – '

'Try and rest. We'll get help soon.'

'I sent you those cards. Both of them. I'm sorry. I saw you in the loo mirror, gazing at my arm. Only a glimpse, but it was enough.'

'But why did you go ahead and cheat if you knew you'd been sussed out?'

'Because I never thought you'd grass on me. But I was wrong.'

'I'm sorry. I never meant to –' Lucy began to cry. 'It was just – just because I was so lonely.'

'I know,' replied Jane. 'I really do understand.'

At last Jane had confessed. It was an incredible relief but Lucy still had the Dark Man to think about. She would have liked to have dismissed him but she couldn't, for Lucy was sure he was still out there, a hovering, menacing presence. 'What about the Dark Man?' she muttered.

'Who?' demanded Jane weakly. 'Who are you on about?'

Then Lucy noticed that Jane was only a metre away from the ivy-covered mound she had seen through the broken window of the coach. The mound she had visited in her dreams.

Hurriedly Lucy began to rip the ivy away in long strands. As she did so, more fire officers as well as police and paramedics began to scramble down into the valley. Lucy went on tearing at the ivy, but she found nothing. No lettering. No gravestone. Only an old tree stump from which a stream of ants was scurrying and scattering.

'What are you doing?' asked Jane, so weak now that she could hardly force out the words.

'Just checking.'

'Checking what?'

'It doesn't matter. Look, the paramedics are coming with a stretcher. You're going to be OK now and they've got the coach shored up too.'

'Will you come to the hospital with me?'

Lucy paused. 'Do you want me to? After all we've been through?'

'Please.' Jane was pleading. 'I need you.'

As the paramedics attended to Jane, Lucy thought she saw a tall, gaunt shadow moving amongst the darkness of the closely packed trees, but she couldn't be sure.

Lucy sat by Jane's hospital bed, holding her hand. Her parents had already arrived, united, at least for a while, in shock, and were sitting outside with Mrs Crow, giving the girls a chance to be together for a short while.

Miraculously no one had been killed in the crash although several students had fractured limbs and Mrs Beacon had severe concussion. Jane herself had escaped with a broken leg and severe bruising, but considering she had been thrown through the window of the coach she had had a lucky escape. They had even managed to remove all the shards of glass from her face.

'Are *you* OK?' whispered Jane.

'Just some cuts and a lot of scratches. They're not even going to keep me in overnight.'

'I'm sorry about those stupid cards.'

'It doesn't matter. It's over.' But is it, wondered

Lucy. She kept remembering the shadow she had seen moving in the woods, and couldn't help worrying that the Dark Man would come again.

'This Ted Turner,' Lucy began.

'I've known him for a long time. He's a nice bloke and he does take messages. He doesn't know what's in them.'

'I'm sure he doesn't,' Lucy replied comfortingly.

'I've lost a lot of friends,' muttered Jane. 'Dawn and Sue are a real drag.'

'You can't go around on your own,' said Lucy anxiously.

'I don't want to.'

'Then –'

'So why don't we go round together again?'

'Us?' Lucy could hardly believe what Jane was saying.

'Yes. Could we be friends again? After all I've done?'

'It's – it's worth a try,' said Lucy, hardly able to believe what Jane had said. 'After all – I did a lot to you too.'

'Can you forgive me?' asked Jane softly.

Lucy squeezed her hand and muttered, 'Isn't it a question of forgiving each other?'

*

That evening, as Lucy was having supper with her parents who amazingly still hadn't exchanged a cross word, there was an urgent ring on the bell. She froze as her mother said, 'If it's that fish and chip man again –'

'I'll go,' said Mr Brent.

'I've just come to see how young Lucy is. It's a miracle no one was killed.' Mrs Jakes was in the kitchen before anyone could stop her, looking excited and tragic at the same time.

'She's very tired,' said Mr Brent, agitatedly following her into the room.

'Lucy. I just wanted to see how you were,' said Mrs Jakes. 'What a miracle you survived.'

Mrs Brent glared at her. 'I thought you were the fish and chip man,' she commented sourly.

Mrs Jakes lowered her eyes and stared rather melodramatically at the floor tiles. 'Funny you should mention him. I saw him on my way back from town. He told me something very sad,' she half-whispered. 'That vagrant who was always hanging around his van. He was found dead in the woods. They think he had a heart attack.'

'How awful,' Lucy muttered.

'Ah well,' Mrs Jakes concluded. 'He doesn't

leave a grieving family. No one seems to know who he was or where he came from.'

'I'm very sorry about this unfortunate tramp, but we mustn't burden Lucy with any more tragedy now,' said Mr Brent abruptly. 'Fortunately the students all survived the coach crash.'

Mrs Jakes nodded and began again. 'That trip should never have gone ahead. Not in this weather and –'

'Thank you so much for coming,' said Mrs Brent icily. She rose to her feet.

As her mother showed Mrs Jakes out, Lucy slowly walked up the stairs with her father.

They both sat on the edge of her bed.

'I'm sorry Mum and I have had so many rows lately,' he said. 'We're really going to try and make a fresh start.' He kissed her and went downstairs.

Friday, 11th

Well, I live to write another entry. And I live to be 13! Tonight I feel safe for the first time all week, but I'm still wondering about that poor vagrant. Who was he? Maybe the police will find out in time. At least I won't dream about the

Dark Man ever again. I'm feeling very sleepy, and all I can think of is what Jane said to me, 'Why don't we go round together?' I feel ecstatic - I really think I might be getting my best friend back, and for the first time in ages it feels as if everything's going to be OK.

13

Lucy woke up suddenly, violently, shaking with the memory of the dream. She'd been walking up the hill again, hand-in-hand with the Dark Man, his grip tight, icy, chilling her to the bone. She had tried to pull away but he wouldn't let go, as they headed for her bleak, cold, snow-covered grave.

Eventually Lucy had pulled so hard that the Dark Man's hand had snapped off. As she huddled under the sheets wide awake, she could feel something wet and pulpy. But when Lucy gazed down under the bedclothes she saw that she was holding her hot water bottle and somehow the stopper had worked loose.

Looking at her bedside clock she saw it was only 2.15 a.m. so she decided to go downstairs to the kitchen, boil a kettle and refill the bottle, making sure the stopper was on properly this time.

Without putting on the landing light so as not to wake her parents, Lucy began to creep down the stairs, but somehow she slipped on the second step. For a split second she wondered if Flo had managed to get into the house again, then she was falling, tumbling down the stairs, rolling to the bottom and bumping her head on the wall. She lay there, slightly stunned, not sure if she was still dreaming.

Woken by the bumping sounds, her mother switched on the landing light and hurried down to her.

'Lucy.' Mum was very agitated. 'Are you all right?'

Lucy sat up, her head aching, nerves screaming. 'Yes. I'm all right, Mum. Don't worry. I'm OK.'

Her mother looked relieved but Lucy wasn't. Could this be a genuine accident, or was the spirit of the Dark Man still after her? The problem was that she would never know. Not till the next time.